The Dead Squirrel

Also by Patrick C. Walsh

The Mac Maguire detective mysteries

The Body in the Boot

The Weeping Women

The Blackness

23 Cold Cases

Two Dogs

The Match of the Day Murders

The Chancer

The Tiger's Back

The Eight Bench Walk

Stories of the supernatural

13 Ghosts of Winter

The Black Vaults Experiment

All available in Amazon Books

Patrick C. Walsh

The Dead Squirrel

The second 'Mac' Maguire mystery

Garden City Ink

A Garden City Ink ebook
www.gardencityink.com

First published in Great Britain in 2015, 2018, 2019
All rights reserved
Copyright © 2015, 2016, 2018, 2019 Patrick C. Walsh

A CIP record for this title is available from the British Library
ISBN 9781984996428

Cover art © Patrick S. Walsh 2015
Thanks to www.cgpgrey.com and shaireproductions.com for the
source images

'*I dislike cruelty, even cruelty to other people, and should therefore like to see all cruel people exterminated*'
 — **George Bernard Shaw**, On The Rocks

For the women who read this story first
Kathleen, Mary and Jean

The Very First Poisoning

He was a man who nobody noticed. He wasn't short or tall, fat or thin, handsome or ugly. In fact, he was so average that he just blended into the background. Being so anonymous would be seen as a sad state of affairs by some but he didn't mind, in fact he didn't mind at all. He lived the interior life of the mind and, while his looks may have been average, his mind most definitely was not.

He first had the idea when he accidentally overheard a conversation about a local scout leader. He investigated and saw for himself. He saw the hot tears of shame that could never be erased from a small boy's face and he knew the truth of it. Years before he'd felt those same tears scalding his own cheeks. The tears had evaporated but the shame remained. It was a ghost that could never be exorcised.

He investigated this loathsome excuse for a human being further. The scout leader was, to all intents, a respectable man. He was a banker, a pillar of the community and, as such, he was above suspicion. He learned that he'd had been reported to the police several times before for 'inappropriate behaviour' with young boys but no action had ever been taken. He felt that it was no coincidence that this particular scout leader was also a member of long standing in a certain secret society and therefore close to some high-ranking police officers.

In his mind he put together a plan, a plan that would make the world a better place. It was just for fun at first. He enjoyed thinking about this man's demise and he knew that the plan he'd crafted and honed would work. It was simple and precise.

He was working in his back garden one morning when he had his epiphany. Some weeks before this part of the

1

garden had looked pitiful as the leaves on all the plants had been ravaged by slugs. He'd laid down some slug pellets and now it was beautiful, regular and pristine and exactly as it should be. He stood there looking at the flower bed for some time.

The world should be the beautiful and pristine too, he thought, but there are too many human slugs out there desecrating the place. They too could do with a pellet.

He stood there and gave this new idea some serious thought. He concluded that he could kill this particular slug and never get caught, he was absolutely sure of it. So, what was stopping him?

He smiled.

Why nothing, nothing at all.

They met for the first and last time in the pub the slug frequented on a Sunday. The slug always drank halves of coke on a Sunday so it was simple. He put his glass down for a few seconds while he told a funny story to his middle-aged, middle-class friends who dutifully grinned and guffawed. He looked at them and wondered if the slug's friends would like him as much if they saw what he got up to behind the scout hut.

He quickly switched glasses and that was that. He walked away and let his friend Mr. T do his work. He didn't change his routine or let himself get curious. A week later he saw it in the local paper, the slug's death notice. Died after a short illness it said. The poison he'd used was a thing of wonder, it was tasteless, colourless and incredibly hard to diagnose. Even harder now as it had been banned for a number of years and people had forgotten all about it.

He saw the slug's funeral. He'd pretended to be visiting another grave and he watched it all out of the corner of his eye. There were only a few mourners there and none of them looked particularly mournful. In fact, the slug's wife seemed quite cheerful considering the circum-stances. He walked out of the cemetery gate with no *expression on his face but inside he felt an electric surge of power that was almost god-like. He revelled in it.*

He had removed one slug but he realised that there were plenty more left who were ripe for extermination.

He allowed himself a smile while he considered who he should introduce Mr T to next.

Chapter One

Mac opened the door to his house and walked inside. The suddenness of the silence waiting inside shocked and unnerved him. His wife hadn't liked silence much. She always had the radio or television on and sometimes she'd sing to herself while she worked. The silence forcefully reminded him once again that his Nora was gone and the pain was once again unbearable.

He'd just spent a week in Birmingham with his sister and some old friends. It had been a good week. He'd laughed a lot and cried a little and he felt as if he'd somehow turned a corner, that he'd finally started to learn to live with his grief.

And now this.

He stood in the hallway frozen, not knowing what to do next. A familiar tiredness started to creep over him. For most of the last six months he'd given in to a deep depression. He'd slept and slept but unfortunately you have to wake up sometime. He knew that he couldn't afford to let the blackness win again.

He suddenly had an idea.

He left his suitcase in the hallway and got some cleaning materials from the kitchen. Then he went into the back garden and opened up the shed. He pulled out one of the folding chairs they used in the garden during the summer. A sudden memory of Nora sitting in the sunlight on such a chair filled his mind. She had a glass of wine in her hand and she was laughing at some joke of his. He somehow managed to hold back the tears and place the chair and the cleaning materials in the boot of his car. He then drove the short distance to the cemetery.

He felt ashamed that he had to search for Nora's grave. He'd only been to the cemetery two or three times since his wife had died. Seeing her name carved in stone just made it all too real for him. After each visit all he'd wanted to do was disappear into sleep and unreality, into a world in his head where he could dream of Nora and pretend that she might still be alive somewhere, somehow.

It was February and still crispy cold. The sun shone down from a clear blue sky and lit up her gravestone. It also lit up the wind-blown dirt. He got out the cleaning spray and cloths and set about making the gravestone as presentable as he could. When he'd finished, he was gratified to see it sparkle in the sunlight. He set up the chair and sat down. He looked around and was glad that no-one else was within earshot.

He felt a little silly when he started but he soon got into full flow. He spoke out loud to his wife and told her all about his trip to Birmingham, who he'd met and what he'd done. He told her how all their relations and friends were doing, all the while leaving gaps for her to respond. The strange thing was he could actually hear her speaking to him in his head. They'd been together so long that he knew exactly what she'd have said. He knew that he was only talking to himself but he found the conversation profoundly comforting none the less.

He became aware of someone approaching a little too late. He turned and saw a middle-aged man who was walking his dog. He was so close that he must have heard Mac speaking out loud to thin air. The man came nearer and was respectfully silent for a while.

'How long is it now?' he simply asked.

'Just over six months,' Mac replied.

The man slowly nodded.

'It's a difficult time, a time when you have to start facing up to things. Mine went two years ago. I get about, still talk to friends and other people I know but the best conversation of the day is still the one I have with my wife.'

He winked at Mac as he walked away.

'Well, Nora,' Mac said after the man had gone, 'I may be going mad but at least I'll have some company.'

When he finished, he promised that he'd visit Nora again soon. When he'd thought of this as he'd stood in the hallway it had seemed silly but, at that moment, he'd felt so desperate that he'd have tried anything. He realised now that it had been one the best ideas he'd ever had. For the first time since his wife had died, he'd felt a sense of her presence and, consequently, felt a lightness in his heart.

Back in the house Mac turned on the radio and selected the music station that Nora used to listen to. He found himself singing along as he unpacked. He looked at his watch, it was just before noon. He knew his friend Tim wouldn't be free until the evening so he decided he might as well go to his office and see if there were any phone messages or post.

As he closed the door behind him, he suddenly noticed the flower beds that fronted the house. He'd always remembered these as being a riot of colour during the spring and summer months. At this time of year Nora would have had it all dug up and the flower seeds already planted. He sighed, now it was just a riot of straggly looking weeds. He was wondering what he should do with it when Amanda Drinkwater came by with her dog.

Mac was tempted to bend down and give the dog a pat but, as his back still a bit sore after all the travelling, he thought better of it.

'Morning, Amanda. I was just wondering what I could do with this,' he said pointing to the flower bed.

He knew Amanda had a beautiful garden, one she looked after all by herself.

'Morning Mr. Maguire,' she said cheerily.

She looked down at the sorry excuse for a flower bed and then at Mac.

'Have you thought of using one of those garden claws?' she asked.

Mac had never heard of them.

'You can weed without having to bend over and with one hand too,' she explained glancing at his crutch.

'One of those sounds just what I need, thanks.'

He'd arranged for a gardener to do all the work in the back garden but he wouldn't be starting for a few weeks yet. Anyway, he liked the idea of being able to do the front flower beds himself.

Amanda looked as if she was about to walk off when she suddenly stopped and turned back.

'Mr. Maguire, I heard that you used to be a policeman but you're a private detective now. Is that right?'

'Yes, that's right, I'm still quite new to it though.'

'Then I was wondering if you could give me some advice.'

Mac gave her a concerned look. He knew that the main reason that most women hired detectives was to get evidence on their wayward husbands. He hoped that she didn't want advice about that. He'd always thought that Amanda and her husband were pretty much the perfect couple.

'Come inside and we'll have a coffee,' he said.

Amanda put her dog in the back garden. Mac got an old dish and put some water in it. The dog, however, was too busy exploring the garden to bother with drinking. Once the coffee was made and they were comfortably seated in the living room Mac took the plunge.

'So how can I help?' he asked, keeping his fingers crossed.

'Mr. Maguire, it's about a poisoning.'

Chapter Two

Mac's face must have shown his surprise.

'So, who's been poisoned?' he asked, trying to think of any recent cases and failing.

'Not who, what. It was a squirrel.'

'A squirrel?' Mac asked, wondering if something had suddenly gone wrong with his hearing.

'Yes, a black squirrel, I found it in my garden a few days ago,' Amanda said as she gave Mac a sad look. 'It died right in front of me. It was convulsing and then it stopped moving a few minutes later, the poor thing. It really upset me if I'm honest. There was something so unnatural about the way it died that I brought it to the local vet and paid him to do an autopsy. He was certain that it hadn't died of any injury so that just left poisoning or disease. In case it was disease he had some tests done at the University. They confirmed that the squirrel had been poisoned.'

'Well they do get in some funny places. They even chewed the electric wiring in my loft once. I'll bet that didn't do them much good. So, what killed it?' Mac asked.

'Something called thallium,' she replied.

Mac's face once again showed his surprise.

'I remember some of the old coppers talking about thallium around the time I joined the force. They said it was wicked stuff, odourless, colourless and deadly. There was a famous case in the early seventies where a serial killer used it to poison members of his own family and even his work mates. He got away with it for ages.'

'I must admit that I'd never heard of it before.'

'There's no reason why you should have,' Mac said. 'It was used in rat poisons and ant killers and that's how most of the murderers who used thallium got hold of it. Thankfully it was banned in the seventies and so it became almost impossible to get. That being the case then how did such a rare poison get into a squirrel in Letchworth?'

'The vet was quite surprised too,' Amanda said. 'He said that he'd be reporting the poisoning but I was wondering if there was something more I should be doing.'

Seeing no immediate reaction from Mac she stood up.

'Oh, I'm just being stupid, aren't I? When I said it was a squirrel just now, I could see that you thought I was mad or something.'

'No, not at all. I'm sorry I was just thinking,' Mac said. 'As I said thallium is wicked stuff. If it's lying around somewhere and a squirrel can get at it then perhaps a child might be able to do so as well. In my opinion it should be found as soon as possible. If it's a case of someone poisoning squirrels on purpose then we still need to find them. They probably have no idea how powerful the poison is and there's more than a good chance that they'll end up poisoning themselves. From what you've said I take it that you haven't gone to the police yet?'

Amanda shook her head.

'I had to get my courage up to ask you. I thought the last thing the police would want to know about was a dead squirrel.'

'Let's go and report it anyway, just in case,' Mac said with a smile. 'It can't do any harm, can it?'

At the police station Mac and Amanda waited patiently in the lobby until a policeman called their names. He led them into an interview room and took their statements. He had a hugely sceptical expression on his face throughout. Amanda was just signing her name when the door opened and a tall woman in a smart trouser suit strode in.

'Mr. Maguire?' she asked.

'Yes, that's me,' Mac replied.

'Would you come with me, please?'

She signed for Amanda to stay where she was.

Mac followed her down a corridor and into another interview room.

'Please wait here,' she said and left him.

He did as he'd been ordered. He was still wondering what it was all about when a tall sandy haired man in his early thirties walked in. Mac did a double take.

'Andy, is that really you?'

The man smiled broadly at Mac.

'Hello boss, how have you been?' he asked, offering his hand.

They shook hands energetically.

'My God, DC Andy Reid! It must be what, five or six years now,' Mac said.

'More like seven and it's DI Andy Reid now.'

'Well done, a Detective Inspector already!'

'You know, I wondered if you'd even remember me,' Andy said. 'After all I was just a Detective Constable the last time we met.'

'How could I forget? You were with the team for two years if I remember right and your work on the Kilburn High Street murders was excellent. Lots of legwork but you persisted and got us that vital break. How's the wife?'

Mac remembered that one of the reasons Andy had left to join the Hertfordshire Police was that he was going to marry a girl from Stevenage.

'She's fine, we've got two kids now, one of each. The best thing I ever did was come here. If I'm honest London was always a bit much for me.'

'I was really sorry to lose you.'

Andy's face showed his pleasure at Mac's words.

'So, what brings you the station today? Are you thinking of joining the force again?' Andy asked.

Mac only wished he could.

'No, I'm here to help someone report an incident... of sorts.'

'An incident? Tell me about it.'

Mac felt a little embarrassed and wished he had something a little more substantial to report than a dead rodent. He told Andy all about it anyway.

'A squirrel?' Andy said, looking totally mystified.

'It's not something I'd normally report but it's the poison that was used that concerns me. Thallium,' Mac said.

'Thallium? Really?' Andy said with a surprised expression. He paused for a moment and was clearly giving it some thought. 'Did you know that there was an epidemic of thallium poisonings in Australia in the fifties and even Agatha Christie used it as a murder weapon in one of her books?'

He'd always been generally impressed with Andy's breadth of knowledge but Mac had the distinct feeling that he'd just looked those facts up. He was very interested to know why.

'Yesterday we dealt with a report of a woman who was found dead in her bed,' Andy said. 'She was in her forties and initially there appeared to be no suspicious circumstances but they did an autopsy anyway.'

'Let me guess,' Mac said, 'our squirrel is the second case of thallium poisoning that you've had today.'

Andy nodded a grim look on his face.

'We received the tox report just a couple of hours ago and they confirmed it. I must admit that I had to look it up on Wikipedia, I've never come across a case of thallium poisoning before.'

'It used to be a really popular murder weapon years ago and probably still would be if it hadn't been banned. The only cases I've heard of in my time were all taken over by the intelligence agencies in the end. So, how come you've now got two reports of thallium poisoning on near enough the same day?'

Andy looked stumped.

'Come on, let's go up to my office.'

Mac popped his head into the interview room and asked Amanda to wait for him. He then gingerly followed Andy up two flights of stairs. Andy sat down at a desk in a large open area. It reminded Mac of where he used to work. Of course, as a Detective Chief Superintendent, he could have had his own office but he'd always liked being surrounded by his team.

Andy introduced the tall woman in the trouser suit. She was in her late thirties, had minimal make-up on and had her hair pulled back into a severe bun. She looked very business-like.

'Mac, this is DS Toni Woodgate.'

They shook hands. Toni's severity softened as she gave Mac a big smile.

'What do we know about the dead woman?' Mac asked.

Andy read aloud from the file he was holding.

'Mrs. Catherine Gascoigne, forty-six, a widow. She'd lived in Letchworth for the past fifteen years or so, ever since she and her husband had moved up from London. Her husband died a few years ago and left her quite a bit of money. Apparently, she was an expert on nineteenth century romantic literature, Jane Austen, the Brontes and the like. She worked at the University as well as teaching a local course here at the Settlement on the Romantic Novelists of the Nineteenth Century. She was also one of the founders of the Letchworth Society of Janeites, whatever that is.'

'How was Mrs. Gascoigne found?' Mac asked.

'Apparently, she'd been off work for a few days as she'd been ill and she'd also missed some important meetings at the Society about an upcoming event. As she was the Chairwoman there were apparently some decisions that could only be approved by her. So, one of the members, a Mrs. Penny Bathurst, volunteered to go and see her. She tried ringing the bell and got no answer so she gained entry with a spare key that she'd been given some time before. She found Mrs. Gascoigne upstairs lying dead on her bed and immediately rang for an ambulance. A couple of uniforms got there some fifteen minutes after the call and, at first sight, it looked like a natural death. Nothing was out of place and there were no signs of forced entry. As it was a sudden death the forensics team were called in, just in case. They reckoned that she'd been dead for at least six hours and they couldn't find any evidence at that point indicating foul play. However, one of the investigators found large clumps of hair on her hairbrush. Apparently, they'd been pulled from her scalp leaving a big gap and that's what got him thinking. He did a special tox screen and that's when the thallium showed up. I spoke to him on the phone and he said that if it hadn't been for the hair it would probably have been put down as a natural death. He also analysed a nearly empty bottle of water that was found on the bedside table. Judging by the concentration of thallium present he said that there would have been enough to kill a horse if she'd drank the whole bottle.'

'You don't think it was suicide though?' Mac asked.

'It's always a possibility I suppose, but no,' Andy replied. 'I think we need to consider this as a murder unless we get any hard evidence to the contrary. Mrs. Bathurst, the woman who found the body, was an old friend and she was very definite that Catherine Gascoigne wouldn't have taken her own life under any circumstances. There was no suicide note but, then again, we don't seem to get that many these days. For me though the real clincher is the poison used. Where on earth would someone like Mrs. Gascoigne get her hands on a sizable quantity of thallium? In fact, why use thallium at all? There are much easier ways to kill yourself if that's what you wanted to do.'

Mac looked thoughtful.

'Did her illness have anything to do with thallium?'

'Almost definitely according to forensics and that's another thing. According to them hair loss usually only happens when thallium has been given over a period and in relatively low doses. Why would you do that and cause yourself unnecessary pain? If you've made the decision to do yourself in, wouldn't you want it to happen as quickly and painlessly as possible?'

'I agree,' Mac said. 'So, it's likely that someone had been poisoning her for a while but the concentration hadn't been strong enough to kill her until she was given a final massive dose. It sounds like our poisoner could be something of an amateur.'

'Or perhaps they wanted to see their victim suffer for a while first,' Toni said with a grim expression.

'You never know. Where did she live?' Mac asked.

'Willian,' Andy replied.

'Willian?' Mac looked puzzled. 'That's miles from where the squirrel died.'

'Exactly, still I can't see it being a coincidence,' Andy said. 'We haven't had any thallium poisonings for God knows how long and now we have two cases, even if one was a squirrel. Anyway, that's pretty much all we know at the moment. We weren't even sure that a crime had been committed until we got the forensic report.'

'So, you haven't started questioning anyone as yet?' Mac asked.

'Not yet, we're still trying to find out who we should contact and, if I'm honest, we're a bit thin on the ground at the moment. We've had a spate of burglaries that's been picked up by the local papers and more than a few councillors have been on our back about it.'

'Yes, I saw the headlines in the paper.'

'Now I suppose I could pull some men off that or...' Andy left the sentence hanging.

Mac smiled broadly.

14

'Need a hand?'

Andy returned the smile.

'This is right up your street, Mac. To be honest I might have paid you a call anyway. I had a meeting with Dan Carter of Luton Police a few days ago and he told me how helpful you'd been in the Hart-Tolliver case. He also told me about your back problems. Do you think you'll be okay?'

Mac assured him that he would be.

'Thanks Andy, boredom and gardening are terrible things and you're saving me from both. So, what's the plan?'

'I was wondering if you'd like to follow up with some of these Janeites,' Andy suggested. 'Hopefully this Penny Bathurst might be able to give you some more information on that. I'll get someone to help you. In the meantime, Toni and I will visit the University and the Settlement and see what we can find out there.'

'What about family? Did she have any?' Mac asked.

'Only distant cousins apparently on her side but there's a sister and brother in law on her husband's side.'

'Mind if I take them as well?' Mac asked.

'Unfortunately, the brother-in-law lives in Canada. I'll try and get him on the phone later today. However, it would help if you could see the sister-in-law. She lives in Baldock so she's not too far away. I've also got the name of Catherine Gascoigne's solicitor. I'm hoping that they might be able to tell us who's in the will. Money's usually a good place to start when there's been a murder.'

'Good thinking, so it looks like we've both got a full day's work ahead of us,' Mac said with a smile.

Andy gave Mac the sister-in-law's address and phone number as well as that of Penny Bathurst. He waited while Andy went to get the 'someone' who would be helping him. He returned with a young girl. She was of medium height and slim-built but with swimmer's shoulders. She wore a brand new black trouser suit with a plain white blouse. Her blond hair was cut short, too short perhaps. She didn't look anywhere near old enough to be a detective. Mac sighed as he realised that everyone was starting to look younger nowadays.

'This is DC Marston,' Andy said. 'She's brand new to the team and she's volunteered to come in a week early for which I'm very grateful as we're so short-handed. She's read the case file so she's as up to date as she can be.'

Mac shook her hand and gave her the once over. She wasn't exactly pretty but she had an interesting face. Mac always thought pretty faces could be very similar but interesting faces were always different. She was smiling but she looked uncomfortable, her eyes flicking from one to the other as they spoke. In her expression he thought he could detect the traces of a little girl who had been let down once too often.

'Okay so we all know what we're doing,' Andy said. 'Let's meet back here around five thirty. We'll go over what we've found and decide what to do next.'

Mac picked up Amanda from the interview room. They walked outside followed by DC Marston.

'I'm sorry to keep you waiting so long but it seems that we were right to report your squirrel's demise after all. Have you ever met a woman called Catherine Gascoigne?' Mac asked.

'No, but I've heard quite a bit about her and the Society,' Amanda replied.

'The Society of Janeites? Go on,' Mac prompted.

'Well they're a group, quite a big group actually, around a hundred members or more I think, and they meet regularly to discuss the works of Jane Austen. They have guest speakers from time to time but the best thing about them is that they hold costume balls every year, one in the Spring and one in Autumn. I'm trying to get tickets to the next one but unfortunately there's always a waiting list. However, I've found this terrific gown, it's blue with little…'

She stopped suddenly and held her hand to her mouth.

'I'm sorry! God, I sounded just like Miss Bates there for a moment.'

'Who's Miss Bates?' DC Marston asked looking quite puzzled.

'A character out of Emma, one of Austen's books,' Mac answered.

Amanda looked at him in surprise.

'I'd never have guessed that you read Jane's books!' she exclaimed.

Mac shrugged. He never let on but he had read one or two of Austen's works. Well, one or two or even six perhaps.

'Anyway, why are you asking me about Catherine Gascoigne? What's she done?' Amanda asked.

'She died,' Mac replied. 'I'm helping the police investigate her death. By the way this is DC Marston who's helping too.'

Amanda gave the young policewoman a smile.

'She died? Really?' Amanda replied her expression turning to one of disbelief. 'I take it that she didn't die naturally then?'

'That's what we think but I'd appreciate it if you kept it to yourself for a while,' Mac asked.

'Of course,' Amanda said. 'Well, I suppose I'd better get going then as you're going to be investigating or whatever. I'll see you later.'

'Amanda, before you go can you tell me how come you know so much about these Janeites?' Mac asked.

'I must admit that I was tempted to join them at one point but a friend of mine who works at the library told me not to bother. She said the woman who ran the

17

Society was a right bitch and so I thought again. She was referring to Catherine Gascoigne.'

'What's the name of your friend?' Mac asked.

'Anne Holding, she runs the local library and she's a mad Jane Austen fan too.'

'How did you meet Anne?'

'I was looking for a novel, my costume fixes my husband calls them,' Amanda replied. 'I mostly read modern stuff but then I go through a phase every three years or so when I really treat myself and read all six of Jane's novels one after the other.'

'She only wrote six novels?' DC Marston asked.

Knowing the author's fame, she looked quite surprised.

'That's all unfortunately but what novels they are!' Amanda replied. 'Anyway, one day I had a craving for some period romance when Anne noticed me skulking around the classics section of the library. She looked at me for a minute and then said, 'I'll bet that you've read all your Austens and you're now looking for something else to keep you going.' I don't know how she knew that but she was spot on. So, we got talking and she told me that she held a little get together every couple of weeks with some other fans to discuss Jane's books and other classical romantic novels and would I be interested?'

'I take it you said yes?' Mac asked.

'Of course, I thought it would be fun. It was at the first meeting that I heard about the Janeites and Catherine Gascoigne. There were five other women in the group besides Anne and me and four of those were ex-members of the Janeites. They all agreed that Catherine Gascoigne was an egotistical cow who considered herself to be a very big fish in Letchworth's small pond. I'm also sure that Anne had some personal reasons for disliking Catherine but she never told me exactly what they were.'

'Thanks for that. Anne Holding sounds like a good place to start,' Mac said.

He said his goodbyes to Amanda who looked wistfully on as Mac and DC Marston walked towards the police car park. She read quite a lot of crime fiction as well as period romances and had always dreamed of getting involved in a real investigation.

'Oh well,' she said.

She sighed a big sigh and went back to get her dog.

Chapter Three

DC Marston glanced up at Mac as they made their way to the car park. She thought that he looked more like an accountant than a policeman and wondered what it would be like working with him.

'So, what do I call you, sir?' she asked.

'Well not 'sir' that's for certain. My name's Mac. What's your first name? If you don't mind that is.'

She hesitated for a split second.

'It's Leigh.'

'Leigh Marston!'

Mac couldn't help smiling.

'What's so funny?' she asked.

He could see that her defences had suddenly come up. As she clearly didn't find his reaction to her name amusing, he tried to explain.

'I'm sorry about that but there's a village just outside Birmingham called Lea Marston. It used to have a big hotel with a French restaurant and years ago it was the place that you took a girl for dinner if you wanted to impress her. I took my wife there a couple of times when we were courting.'

'Really?' was all she replied.

'I think the food might have impressed her but my French definitely didn't,' Mac said trying to lighten things a little.

Leigh said nothing and still looked quite put out.

The smell of books hit Mac as he and Leigh walked inside the library. It immediately brought him back in time to the red-bricked Victorian palace of a library he'd almost lived in when he was young. Ghost stories had been his favourite back then. He remembered reading them aloud to his friends by a flickering candle in the gang's hideout, in reality his father's garden shed, and nearly scaring each other to death. He tended to buy all his books online now, something he suddenly thought was probably a bit of a shame.

He asked at the counter for Anne Holding and the librarian pointed down an aisle to a figure placing books on a shelf.

The figure turned as they approached and a smile broke out on her face. Anne Holding was in her forties and had a somewhat rounded figure. Mac thought it suited her though, she looked like a very pleasant woman indeed.

'Can I help you?' she asked with a smile.

'We're from the police,' Mac said as he introduced himself and Leigh.

Her smile went down a notch as Leigh showed her a warrant card.

'How can I help the police?' she asked.

Mac wondered why she suddenly appeared to be so nervous. Did she have something to hide?

'We just need to ask a few questions. Can we sit down somewhere, away from the public areas?' he asked.

'Sure, follow me.'

She led them towards the back of the library and on the way had a word with another librarian.

'Just making sure someone's looking after the shop.'

She opened the door into a room that was used as a kitchen. It had a small table and four plastic chairs.

'Will this do? It's where we have our lunch.'

Mac could see that her hands were trembling slightly.

'This will be fine,' Mac assured her.

They all sat down. Mac thought Anne looked agitated and was clearly worried about something.

'Tell me, why do you think we've come here today?'

'It's...it's not my husband, is it?' she asked nervously.

'No, it's nothing to do with your husband.'

Anne sat back with a looked of utter relief on her face.

'I'm sorry, I thought you might be going to tell me something terrible about my husband. I've had this dream quite a few times where someone official comes into the library and it's always bad news.'

'We're looking for some information on Mrs. Catherine Gascoigne. But before we go on tell me why you're so worried about your husband?'

'He's in the Army, he's a staff sergeant and he's just been sent back to the Middle East as part of a humanitarian mission,' Anne replied. 'Of course, he was all up for it, the idiot still thinks he's twenty. He's due to retire in a couple of years but I wish to God it was right now.'

She looked upwards and muttered a little prayer.

She collected herself and then looked levelly at Mac and asked, 'So what do the police want to know about the wicked witch of the west?'

Mac told her about Catherine Gascoigne's death.

'She's dead? Really?'

Anne's face clearly showed her disbelief.

'I take it that there's something suspicious about it if you're asking questions?' she asked.

'You could say that. Please keep it to yourself but she was poisoned.'

'Poisoned? Now I really find that really hard to believe, I mean this is Letchworth not mediaeval Rome.'

'Who might have wanted her dead?' Mac asked.

'A lot of people that I could think of,' she replied. 'To be honest if they formed a queue they'd probably go around the block.'

'Why is that? Why was Mrs. Gascoigne so disliked?'

'She thought the world revolved around her, it always had to be about her and she was a bit of a bully too. She ran the Society like it was her personal little kingdom, making sure that only her cronies got elected. Anyone who disagreed with her was shown the door one way or another.'

'What do you mean by 'one way or another'?' Mac asked.

'Well, usually there'd be an unscheduled meeting, always when Catherine had a healthy majority of her cronies present of course. Then you'd be voted out, expelled from the Society. It must have happened three or four times while I was a member.'

'Is that what happened to you?' Mac asked.

She paused for a second. Obviously, the memory wasn't a good one.

'No, I resigned.'

'Why?'

'It was a case of plagiarism, Mr. Maguire.'

Mac could see real anger in Anne's face.

'That's tantamount to a crime in our circles,' she continued. 'Let me explain, for a while I've had this theory about why Wickham elopes with Lydia...'

'Pride and Prejudice,' Mac explained seeing the baffled look on Leigh's face.

'That's right. Well, Wickham was in a tight spot. He had huge gambling debts and, in all probability, some not very nice people chasing after him for money. So, I always thought it was a bit unlikely that he'd just run off with a more or less penniless young girl. I think that Wickham's problem was that he wanted to be Darcy, all his life he'd been eaten up by jealousy of the man he'd been brought up with. Anyway, I had this theory that Wickham had a spy in Meryton, perhaps even in Longbourn itself, as I wouldn't have put it past him to have seduced one of the maids. Anyway, this spy would have let him know that Elizabeth Bennett was going to Derbyshire and not to the Lake District as originally planned.

He knew that Darcy was still mad about her so he gambled on Darcy and Elizabeth meeting up again and that's why he eloped with her younger sister Lydia. Always the gambler he was hoping that he would get some advantage out of the situation and he was right, wasn't he? Once Darcy found Wickham and Lydia he more or less bribed Wickham to marry her which was exactly what Wickham wanted anyway in my opinion. He got a commission in the army and all his debts paid off which would have cost quite a sum back then. Not only that but he knew that, if his plans worked out, he'd actually be related to Darcy through marriage and have a meal ticket for life.'

'I hadn't thought of it in that way,' Mac said. 'You're right, Wickham would have a sort of permanent revenge.'

'You seem to know Jane's books very well. You're not a secret Janeite yourself are you Mr. Maguire?' Anne enquired with a smile.

'Well, I've been known to read the odd one,' he replied with some understatement. 'Please go on.'

'Anyway, one evening after having a glass or two of wine I mentioned this to Catherine and she asked me if I was going to publish. I said that I might but I wanted to develop the thought a little first. Then a week later I saw an article she wrote entitled 'Who was Wickham's spy at Longbourn?' It was my little theory blown into something much bigger and, of course, my name wasn't mentioned at all.'

'I'll bet that you were quite upset about that,' Mac stated.

'Upset? Fuming was more like it. I confronted her after one of the meetings and she pretended not to understand. Bloody brazen she was. Of course, I'd never written anything down and so I couldn't prove a thing. I resigned and that was that.'

'If I'm honest you don't strike me as the type of person who'd take something like that lying down,' Mac said.

'Normally you'd be right but I didn't want to push it too far so I just kept it to myself.'

Mac was puzzled.

'Why would you do that?'

'I suppose I didn't want to make an enemy of her in case in case she barred me from the balls. They're still the high points of the year for me.'

'What exactly are these balls?' Mac asked remembering that Amanda had mentioned them earlier.

Anne's face lit up.

'Oh, they're so beautiful and so romantic. They take place in the ballroom in the Spirella building, it's such a fantastic room for a costume ball. I've got two different dresses, both absolutely authentic for the period, one for Spring and one for Autumn, and my husband looks splendid in his uniform. It's based on the militia uniform in Pride and Prejudice.'

'Your husband goes too?' Mac asked with some surprise.

'I think he secretly likes it as much as I do. It's very romantic and the romance doesn't stop with the ball if you know what I mean.'

She gave Mac a cheeky wink.

'Oh, and the music is so beautiful too. There's a string quartet playing the very same music that Jane herself might have danced to, the lights are always low and there's as many candles as health and safety will allow. It's decorated exactly as a ballroom in Jane's time would have been and its always different depending on which ball they choose.'

'I take it that they theme them on the balls in the books?' Mac asked.

'Oh yes, the one coming up is the Spring ball and that's based on the Netherfield ball where Darcy first dances with Elizabeth. Now last Autumn's ball was based on the Lower Rooms in Bath where Catherine meets Mr. Tilney, and last Spring's was...'

Anne stopped and suddenly looked quite sad.

'Was what? Why did you stop?' Mac asked.

'It was based on the ball at The Crown in *Emma*. I'm sorry but some memories of that ball are not so pleasant to me.'

Mac leant forward.

'Tell me.'

'It was all going so well when, on my way to the toilets, I saw Catherine insisting on calling poor Pippa 'Miss Bates' and then she took her to one side and said something to her. Unfortunately, with the music being so loud, I couldn't hear exactly what Catherine said but it must have said something really cutting because Pippa was in absolute bits afterwards. She left the ball in tears and the next day she was found in her house hanging from a light fitting. We found out later that she'd had a history of mental health problems but I still think it was that cow that pushed her over the edge.'

'Did anyone else think that?' Mac asked.

'There was only Catherine and her two cronies there. I'm not sure if anyone else saw what happened, if they did, they've kept it to themselves.'

'What was Pippa's full name and what else can you tell me about her?'

Mac thought that a suicide in those circumstances might well provide someone with an excellent motive for murder.

'Philippa Hatch,' Anne replied. 'She must have been in her forties I suppose, a thin slip of a woman. I don't think anyone could say that they really knew her. She was very quiet and hardly ever spoke at the meetings but she was absolutely brilliant at making these little accessories that we all wear in our hair for the balls. They're very authentic and made out of silk flowers, ribbons and pearls. She gave us all one and they were really beautiful. I remember when she gave me mine, she was really shy at first, but then she gave me the most wonderful smile when I said how much I liked it. Unfortunately, anyone could have seen that she lived on her nerves but she so loved the Society and the balls until...'

'Did she have any family, a husband?'

'Not as far as I know. There were only members or ex-members of the Society at her funeral. That's sad, isn't it?'

Mac was thoughtful for a while. If she didn't have anyone who was close to her then it was unlikely that the poisoning was in revenge for her suicide. None the less he made a mental note of it.

'Tell me about the Janeites,' Mac asked. 'Who'll be running the Society now that Mrs. Gascoigne is dead?'

'I'm not sure to be honest. By rights it should be Tanya Stokes as she's Deputy Chairperson.'

'Was she close to Mrs. Gascoigne?'

'No, not especially, she wasn't one of Catherine's cronies if that's what you mean. As Deputy she really had nothing to do as Catherine did everything herself. I think letting Tanya get voted in was just a sop to the Janeites who disliked her.'

'Who were her cronies then?'

'There were quite a few who sucked up to her but her closest allies would be the 'gruesome twosome', Olivia Parker and Penny Bathhurst,' Anne replied. 'Olivia's the Treasurer and Penny's in charge of events, the balls in other words.'

'Is there anyone else we should speak to?'

Anne shrugged.

'Everyone and no-one really. The Society still has well over a hundred members and I'm sure that for quite a few of those Catherine's passing will be cause for celebration. A ball without Catherine, now that will be absolute bliss Mr. Maguire. I only hope that my husband can get back home in time for it.'

'Who keeps the list of members?' Mac asked.

'Olivia I should think as she's the treasurer. She lives just around the corner on Broadway.'

She told him the house number.

'Is there anything else you can tell me?' Mac asked.

Anne slowly shook her head.

'I must admit that, while theoretically I thought I'd be dancing for joy at the news, in reality I actually find it quite shocking.'

'If you do think of anything else please call me on this number.'

He wrote down his mobile number and passed it to her.

Outside Leigh looked at Mac with a puzzled expression.

'Do you really read Jane Austen?' she asked.

'Yes, why?'

She just shook her head and didn't answer.

'Do you think that Philippa Hatch's suicide might have a bearing on the murder?' she continued.

'Well, it might provide someone with a very good motive, if there was anyone who'd been close to her that is. Remind me to look her file up when I get back to the station.'

Mac stopped and looked at Leigh.

'Andy said that you were new to the team. It's not your first day by any chance?' he asked.

She nodded. She had a little smile on her face but it couldn't have been sadder.

That explained a lot, Mac thought, but perhaps not quite everything. He felt that there was some sort of shadow hanging over his new colleague and this made her even more interesting.

Mac was curious and he promised himself that he'd try and find out what made her tick.

Chapter Four

Anne hadn't been wrong about Olivia Parker living just around the corner, it took them less than a minute to drive there. The house was barn-sized with three huge bow windows on the ground floor and two more on the first floor. Outside there was enough space to park a couple of large articulated lorries but there was only an old green Range Rover in evidence at the moment.

He rang the doorbell and a few minutes later the door was opened by a dumpy middle-aged woman in a floral dress who was dabbing her eyes with a handkerchief. Mac guessed that this was Mrs. Parker and that she'd already heard about her friend's demise.

Leigh showed the woman her warrant card.

'We're investigating the death of Mrs. Catherine Gascoigne,' Mac said.

The woman said nothing and just waved at them with her handkerchief to follow her inside. Mac looked around. There was a lot of wood, ceiling beams, wooden panels, wooden columns, tables and ladder-back chairs, a forest's worth at least. The furniture was Arts and Crafts style and he guessed that most of it was genuine and around a hundred years old. Someone definitely had money.

The woman led them to a table set into one of the bow windows and gestured for them to sit down.

'I take it that you're Mrs. Olivia Parker?' Mac asked.

The woman nodded and then dabbed at an eye with her handkerchief.

'How did you hear about Catherine Gascoigne's death?' Mac asked.

'Penny told me yesterday. She rang me while she was waiting for the police and ambulance to arrive. Oh, I can't believe it Mr. Maguire, such a bright, vibrant light, now extinguished like a spent match.'

Mac thought that her turn of phrase was a bit theatrical.

'Can you shed any light on who might have wanted Mrs. Gascoigne dead?'

Mrs. Parker looked stunned and then horrified.

'What are you saying? Are you telling me that Catherine was murdered?'

'Yes, I'm afraid it's quite likely that she was,' Mac replied. 'Did she have any enemies, anyone who hated her enough to want to kill her?'

Mrs. Parker looked insulted.

'No, no of course not. Catherine was a determined person, she had to be or nothing would have been done, but she was always kind. She was a saint really. I just can't imagine anyone wanting to kill her.'

She started crying again. Mac gave her a minute.

'Tell me about Catherine and the Janeites. How did it all get started?' he asked.

'When it started some twelve years ago it was just Catherine, Penny, myself and a few friends. We didn't call ourselves a Society back then we were just 'Janeites'. We started meeting regularly and word got around. It grew slowly over the years but it really took off when Catherine had the brilliant idea of holding a costume ball. We based it on the first one in Pride and Prejudice, you know where Darcy turns down the chance to dance with Elizabeth. Anyway, it was a roaring success, as were most of Catherine's projects, and ever since the balls have been immensely popular. There's been a waiting list for tickets every year since we started. Members get first dibs of course.'

'I believe that Mrs. Gascoigne wasn't popular with everyone though?'

She pursed her lips as she said, 'Well some people are never satisfied, are they? We let them become part of the Society and then they want to take it over and do things their way. It's our Society not theirs. And as for that horrible Mrs. Holding she even accused Catherine of plagiarism once, I heard her.'

She gave Mac a look of great indignation.

'And did she?'

'Catherine would never do anything like that. Anyway, it's all you'd expect from people like that, total ingratitude, and after we'd allowed her to join the Society too.'

'What do you mean by 'people like that'?'

Mac was asking but he was fairly sure he knew the answer.

She gave Mac a sideways glance.

'Well you know...'

'You mean because she's black.'

'Exactly,' she said taking Mac's even temperament for agreement.

She leant forward conspiratorially.

'They all have a chip on their shoulder and I never understood why she wanted to join the Society in the first place. In Jane's novels her people would at best be holding the horses, wouldn't they?'

Mac decided that he really disliked Olivia Parker. He did his best to not let it show though, he needed to get as much out of her as possible.

'What about Philippa Hatch? Tell me what you know about her.'

'Pippa? I think there was something wrong with her up here, the poor dear.'

She tapped the side of her head as she spoke.

'She was one of those overly nervous women. I never saw her happy, she was just an accident waiting to happen in my opinion.'

'Is it true that Catherine upset her the night she killed herself?' Mac asked.

She gave him a look designed to show indignation but instead Mac thought it reeked of defensiveness.

31

'No of course not. I'll bet it was that Mrs. Holding who told you that lie, wasn't it?'

'It's not a lie though, is it?'

Mac gave her his best stare and held her eyes for as long as he could.

She looked away first.

'Well what if she was upset? Catherine was only joking but Pippa was just like Miss Bates and took everything to heart.'

'What did Catherine say to her?' Mac asked.

'Nothing really. She was just acting the part and asked Pippa how her mother was and hoped she'd be happy at Mr. Woodhouse's for the evening, something along those lines, I think. She was pretending that Pippa was Miss Bates you see.'

'Are you sure that was all? Whatever she said really upset Philippa,' Mac said.

'I could see that she was getting a little hot under the collar but God alone knows why. It wasn't anything we did.'

Mac's face clearly showed his scepticism.

'We didn't bully that poor woman if that's what you're thinking,' she said.

'We have a witness that says differently.'

She looked angrily at Mac but said nothing. She stood up and looked out of the window.

'I want you to leave now.'

'I'll go but not before I get a full list of members and ex-members of the Society.'

She turned and said, 'I don't keep ex-member's details. Catherine said something about data protection so, when a member leaves, I just delete the whole record.'

'What do you use to record members' details?' Mac asked.

She led Mac and Leigh into an alcove which contained a computer desk with a laptop on it.

'That.'

'I'll need to borrow your laptop then,' Mac said.

'My laptop?' Mrs. Parker looked both indignant and nervous at the same time. 'No, that's absolutely impossible.'

'Are you refusing? May I remind you that this is a murder investigation.'

'Do what you like, you're not having it,' she said defiantly.

Mac's face showed his annoyance.

'Mrs. Parker, I don't understand. The woman who you say was your friend is dead and that laptop could hold vital evidence as to who killed her,' he said in his sternest voice.

She said nothing.

'Okay, if you don't comply then I'll put a police guard on it and be back here in half an hour with a court order.'

'Do you know who my husband is?' she shrieked.

'Mrs. Parker, I wouldn't care if your husband was the Chief Constable. I'm going to ask you just one more time. Can we please have your computer?'

Even Mac was shocked when she picked up the laptop, held it high over her head and smashed it hard on to the parquet wooden floor. She then jumped up and down on it several times.

'There you are, you can have it now if you still want it,' she shouted.

Bits of the laptop were spread across the floor.

'Make sure that she doesn't touch anything,' he told Leigh.

He went out into the hallway and made a call. He returned and stood silently by the smashed laptop looking steadily at Mrs. Parker without a flicker of emotion. She turned away and looked out of the window. A few minutes later a blue light could be seen flashing through the front windows. Mac answered the door and two uniformed police followed him in.

'Mr. Maguire, what do you need?' asked one of the policemen.

'Can you put what's left of this into a bag and take it to one of your forensic computer specialists. I take it that you have some of those?'

'Of course, sir. They're stationed in the Welwyn headquarters,' the officer replied.

'Okay, the owner has agreed that we can have it so get the laptop to Welwyn as quickly as possible. Tell the specialist that we want everything that's on the hard drive and to send the information to DI Andy Reid at Letchworth station. Tell them that it's a murder investigation and top priority.'

Mac and Leigh stood by while the policemen picked up every bit of the smashed laptop and placed them into several large evidence bags which they then sealed.

When they'd gone Mrs. Parker said acidly, 'I don't know why you're bothering, that won't ever work again.'

Mac smiled and this seemed to unnerve her.

'It doesn't need to. I doubt you've done any real damage to the hard drive, that's the computer's memory. I've worked with a few of these specialists and the things they can do are almost magical. We once rescued a computer from a fire. Parts of it had actually melted but they still got all of the information it held, every key stroke made and of course every deleted document because nothing ever gets truly deleted on a hard drive. Thank you very much for your co-operation,' he said with a straight face.

He glanced back on his way out to see a very worried looking woman watching them leave. Mac suddenly became quite interested in finding out what that hard drive might contain.

Chapter Five

'Meeting Mrs. Parker might help us to paint a better picture of Catherine Gascoigne, don't you think?' Mac asked as they got into the car. 'Someone once said that you can often judge a person by their friends.'

'Well, after meeting just one of them I think I can safely say that this Catherine must have been a right cow,' Leigh stated.

'Come on, let's see what this Penny Bathurst has got to say for herself.'

They pulled up outside a house even bigger that the one they'd just left. The door was answered by a young Filipino woman dressed as a maid in a black dress and frilly white apron. Mac showed her his warrant card.

'Can you please tell Mrs. Bathhurst that we need to speak to her.'

The maid left without speaking, closing the door behind her. Mac glanced around at Leigh.

'Are they filming a Poirot in there or something?' she asked incredulously.

She gave him a smile as she said this. He thought it suited her.

A minute or so later the door opened a crack.

'Go away, I don't want to talk to you, I'm too upset.'

The door slammed shut again.

'Mrs. Bathurst,' Mac shouted loudly at the door. 'There's been a murder and I need to talk to you. If you refuse then I'll be forced to arrest you and we'll talk at the station. It's your decision.'

They waited over two minutes before the door opened and a very tall, thin woman in her late forties appeared.

She'd reconsidered and waved at them to follow her inside. Another forest of wood awaited them inside. Mrs. Bathurst was waiting for them in a room so big that they could have played a tennis match in it and still had room for the spectators. She stood next to a long dining table that could have accommodated at least twenty people but she made no move to sit down. As she didn't, neither did Mac or Leigh.

She had a dazed look on her face as she said, 'Olivia just rang and she told me that Catherine was murdered. I just can't believe it. I mean people don't get murdered in Letchworth, at least not anyone I'm likely to know.'

Mac looked up to her. He had to as she must have been at least six inches taller than him.

'Mrs. Bathurst, you're the one who found Catherine Gascoigne dead. Don't you want us to catch her murderer?' he asked.

She thought on this and then said, 'Yes, yes of course I do. I'm sorry, I'm being a fool. Go on then, ask your questions.'

'Have you any idea who might have wanted to kill Catherine Gascoigne?'

She shook her head.

'I know that some people didn't get on with her but do I know anyone who hated her enough to kill her? No, I just can't see it being one of the Janeites.'

'What about ex-Janeites?' Mac asked.

'Same there really, I know some of them disliked Catherine. I'll admit that Catherine was...well, a bit difficult at times. She definitely liked things her own way but, as far as I was concerned, her way was usually the right one. No-one knew her like we did. We were all at boarding school together and she looked after Olivia and me. No-one bullied us when she was around. The Three Musketeers we used to call ourselves. I'll really miss her.'

'Yes, there's a big difference between not getting on with someone and hatred, hatred is much more personal, isn't it? Is there anything else you can tell me that might give us a clue?' Mac asked.

Penny shook her head again.

'I'm sorry, nothing comes to mind.'

'What about Philippa Hatch?'

'What about her? You don't think someone killed Catherine because of mousy little Pippa Hatch, do you?' Penny replied disdainfully. 'Catherine was just mildly poking fun at her when the stupid girl burst into tears and ran off. Next thing we know she'd gone and killed herself. In my opinion whatever pushed her into doing such a mad thing had nothing to do with Catherine or any other Janeite come to that.'

'So, you can't think of anything that might help us?'

'That's all I've been doing since Catherine died, thinking, thinking but there's nothing...'

'Did anything unusual happen over the past few weeks? Even the smallest thing might help,' Mac asked.

'No, not really...well, I doubt it's relevant, but Catherine did say that she ran into some woman when she out running. That's all I can honestly remember.'

'Tell me more,' Mac said.

'Well, she was out running when she collided with this woman. It was all Catherine's fault apparently, she said. She'd been listening to music on her headphones and wasn't really paying attention. Anyway, the woman didn't seem to be hurt so they brushed themselves off and left it at that.'

Mac gave this some thought.

'Did Catherine carry one of those water bottles you see runners with these days?'

Penny thought for a few seconds.

'Yes, yes she did. A purple one if I remember rightly. I sometimes joined her but I couldn't do it every other day like Catherine.'

'Where and when did the collision take place?'

'Somewhere on Letchworth Gate just before she turned right down Baldock Lane going back towards Willian.

She pointed out the spot as we drove by last Monday. The collision happened the day before.'

'Had Catherine ever collided with anyone else before when she'd been out running?' Mac asked.

'Not as far as I know and I'm sure she'd have mentioned it if she had.'

'Where were you going when Catherine pointed out where the collision took place?'

'We were going to look at some decorations for the ball,' Penny said. 'I had to drop her home early though as she had a bad stomach. It had been bothering her for a while but she wouldn't see a doctor, would she? She seemed so self-reliant but, in reality, she was scared stiff of medical people. We had this bitch of a nurse at school who... oh well, that's another story.'

'How long had Catherine had this bad stomach for?' Mac asked.

'A couple of weeks on and off. After we pleaded with her, she eventually went to a doctor and got something for it. It seemed to help and, for a while at least, she was back to her old self.'

'Thank you, Mrs. Bathurst,' Mac said. 'You've been really helpful.'

'Have I? Well I hope you catch whoever did this soon, Olivia and I are afraid to leave the house.'

'You should be. Whoever killed Catherine might be after you two as well,' Mac said. 'Stay indoors and be careful what you eat and drink, is that clear?'

Penny's face went suddenly white.

'Are you being serious, Mr. Maguire?'

'I've never been more so and make sure Olivia Parker gets the message too. Here's my number, if either you or Mrs. Parker think of anything else please ring me immediately.'

Mac was thoughtful as he stood on the pavement. Leigh was surprised to see him turn and go back and once again knock on the door. The maid answered.

'Please ask Mrs. Bathurst to come back to the door.'

A few seconds later she appeared.

'Have you forgotten something, Mr. Maguire?'

'Just one more question. How hard would it be to get into Mrs. Gascoigne's house?'

'Well, easy for me as I have a spare key. Otherwise it's quite secure, locks on all the windows and it's well protected with a burglar alarm.'

'People sometimes leave a spare key under the mat or a flower pot,' Mac said. 'Did she ever do anything like that?'

'Yes actually, she usually left a key under a stone, the cleaner was always misplacing hers and Catherine didn't like her missing a day. She really couldn't stand any mess at all.'

'Did any of the Janeites know about this key?' Mac asked.

'Perhaps, let me think. Yes, it was last year and Molly Etherington was looking for somewhere to store some of the decorations for the ball. I overheard Catherine tell her about the key. She said she'd be at work and that Molly was to let herself in.'

'I take it that Catherine also told her the code for the burglar alarm?'

'Yes, I suppose that she must have done.'

'Do you know where this Molly Etherington lives?'

'No, I'm sorry, I don't,' Penny said.

'I take it that you know the code to the burglar alarm?'

'Yes of course, I've got it here somewhere.'

She went inside and a minute later returned with a slip of paper. Mac looked at the paper and thought how stupid intelligent people could sometimes be. Mac thanked her and they left.

'What was all that about?' Leigh asked.

'I'll tell you in a minute. Let's drive to Letchworth Gate.'

Letchworth Gate was the main road into the town from the A1 motorway. Mac told Leigh where to stop and told her to park the car half onto the grass verge so that the traffic could get by. He got his crutch out of the back.

'So, what are we looking for?' Leigh asked.

'If I'm honest I'm not too sure. I just wanted to see the lay of the land that's all.'

Mac stood and looked up and down the road. A thin strip of asphalt pavement ran next to the grass verge and beyond that were clumps of decorative bushes and trees.

'I can see why Catherine wasn't expecting to bump into anyone, there's only the motorway at that end,' Mac said.

'But there's a pedestrian crossing not far away so someone must use it,' Leigh observed.

'Yes, if I remember right there's a footpath that runs parallel to Baldock Lane. It's mostly people from the estate over the other side of the road who use it for walking their dogs. I guess that it might be good for runners too as it's away from the traffic.'

Mac stood there for a few minutes as he looked up and down the road.

'So, what are we looking for?' Leigh asked.

Mac thought she sounded a little exasperated.

'I think there's a good chance that the collision wasn't an accident. It's possible that the woman who Catherine collided with hid behind a bush or a tree and then jumped into her path. Of course, Catherine would automatically think it was her fault.'

'But what would that achieve?'

'It would get more poison into Catherine, that's what,' Mac said. 'Most running equipment I see these days seem to have the maker's logo on it, it's a status thing like designer labels, isn't it? If it were me, I'd watch and take a photo of Catherine in secret, then go online and buy a water bottle of exactly the same type and colour. Fill it up with water and the poison and then switch the bottles in the seconds after the collision.'

'That's clever,' Leigh said, 'but mightn't the water levels in the two bottles be different?'

'That's a good point,' Mac replied giving her a smile.

Leigh looked quite pleased with herself.

'However, if you assume that she filled her bottle when she started her run then you might be able to get it near enough. Didn't Penny Bathurst say that Catherine turned back here towards Willian? That would make this around the halfway mark. I wonder....'

Mac fell silent for a quite a while. Leigh began to wonder what she'd been landed with.

'Wonder what?' she eventually asked.

Mac came back from wherever he'd been.

'I'm sorry, I was thinking about water levels. If this is around the half way mark then whoever poisoned Catherine could only put a little over half the liquid in the bottle. But what if Catherine didn't drink it all? I've often thought that a lot of these runners who carry water bottles do it more for show. I was just wondering if that was how the murderer might have gotten the dose wrong again and that's the reason why Catherine didn't die straight away.'

'Wrong dose again? What do you mean?' Leigh asked.

'From what Mrs. Bathurst said, and also from the forensics evidence, it's likely that Catherine Gascoigne had been given multiple doses of poison over a period of a few weeks and this was the reason for her stomach problems. So, either the killer wasn't sure of the lethal dose or they wanted her to suffer first. I'm not so sure about that last one though.'

'Why? If someone hated her enough to kill her wouldn't they have wanted her to suffer too?' Leigh said.

'Possibly but it's very risky, isn't it?' Mac replied. 'There's an antidote to thallium and, if Catherine had been seen by a doctor who had recognised the symptoms, then her life might have been saved. Not only that but an investigation into a case of attempted murder would automatically follow and there'd be a very real risk that the poisoner might get caught. So, if the poisoner wanted her dead why take that chance? By far the safest course would be to give her a lethal dose and hope that it gets put down to natural causes, that way there's no investigation and no risk. Anyway, it's my guess that the poisoner came back again and made sure Catherine got the proper dose this time.'

It was now Leigh's turn to be thoughtful.

'I guess that's why you asked about getting into Catherine's house. You think the killer knew about the spare key.'

'Spot on. Come on, let's go there next and see what we can see.'

Catherine's house was a large black and white half-timbered house near the crossroads in Willian. It stood at the end of a short drive and was at ninety degrees to the main road. A sign by the door said 'The Old Alms House Anno Domini 1641'.

Mac asked Leigh to get some plastic evidence bags and a marker pen from the boot of the car.

'Now, you need to find a loose stone not far from the front door, one big enough to hide a key. If you don't mind, I'll leave this one to you. I'm not so good at bending down these days.'

Leigh gave him a long look.

'Do you mind me asking why?'

'No, actually I don't mind at all.'

In fact, Mac was quite pleased she'd asked. Most people didn't and Mac had a little theory about that.

'I have a lower spinal condition that leaves me in constant pain. I have to be careful and make sure I don't do too much or it just makes the pain worse. So, bending over can be a major problem at times. A while back I dropped my keys, bent down to pick them up and ended up in bed for two days.'

'Okay,' she replied apparently happy with Mac's explanation.

It took Leigh less than five minutes to find the key. She carefully manoeuvred the stone into the plastic bag without touching it then she sealed the bag and wrote the date, time and the location of the find. He could see the key lying in the shallow indentation left by the stone. Leigh picked it up by using a pen then she placed the key into another plastic bag and wrote on that too. She handed both bags to Mac. He looked closely at the key and then placed both bags in his pocket.

Leigh was puzzled.

'Why are you putting the key in your pocket? I thought we were going in the house for a look around?'

'We are.'

'Yes, but that only means you'll need to get the key out again to open the door.'

He gave her a mysterious smile.

They walked together towards the front door. Mac removed the crime scene tape. Leigh stood behind him as he surreptitiously pulled out a bunch of lock picks from his jacket pocket. He inserted a couple of picks and no more than ten seconds later the door was open. Mac could hear electronic beeps as the alarm started counted down. He quickly found the burglar alarm terminal and entered the code. The beeping stopped.

'So how on earth did you do that?' Leigh asked in some wonder.

'Lock picks,' Mac replied showing her the bunch of picks. 'I like to keep in practice.'

'How did you learn to do that then? I didn't see any courses on lock picking when I was at Police College.'

'An old copper taught me not long after I became a detective. I was the youngest in the team and at the time I seemed to spend most of my time making tea. This old copper told me to practice in my spare time as it would be a very useful skill to have and he was absolutely right.'

'Forgive me but I'm finding this quite strange,' Leigh said. 'I normally know something about the people I work with but I find that I know nothing about you except, of course, that you like Jane Austen and that you'd make a pretty good burglar.'

'It's the finding out that's the real fun,' Mac said with a wink. 'Come on, let's have a look inside.'

Catherine's house was quite a bit smaller than Olivia Parker's and Penny Bathurst's but it also had a lot less clutter. In fact, to Mac's surprise it had no clutter at all. This gave him an idea. They looked around the downstairs rooms; a lounge, a dining room, a TV room, a small office space and the kitchen which was quite large.

'This is really nice!' Leigh exclaimed.

'Why?' Mac asked.

'Do you really want to know?' she asked.

'Absolutely, I've always found that a house can tell you a lot about the people who live there or person as in this case.'

'Well...' Leigh looked around the rooms again while Mac followed after her. 'It's all absolutely spotless and, although I know that she had a cleaner, I'd bet that she cleaned this place herself as well. There's not a thing even slightly out of place as far as I can see. It's quite minimal but the furniture is very good quality and the colours all go together beautifully. I have to admit that overall she's done a great job. I definitely wouldn't mind living here.'

'Interesting, so you like blue too.'

Again, Mac was thoughtful for a while.

'It could be just that she had an eye for detail but it could also be something else,' he said. 'Come on, let's look upstairs.'

44

There were three large bedrooms. One was used as a lumber room and was full of boxes, all numbered and neatly positioned in rows. Mac noticed that there was no dust on any of the boxes. The second bedroom smelt faintly of tobacco. The bed was made and the duvet had been turned back. There was a pair of men's slippers under the bed and a dressing gown hung on the back of the door.

'Her dead husband's room, I'd guess,' Leigh said.

'Yes, I believe it's been a couple of years since he died but it looks as though he just stepped out a minute or two ago.'

Leigh touched the top of the bedside table with her finger.

'No dust, so she cleans in here regularly too.'

The last bedroom was Catherine's.

'So, this is where she died,' Leigh said.

'Yes, I believe they found the bottle of water here, on the bedside table.'

They both looked around the room. Mac opened a large wardrobe and looked at it for some time.

'Come here and have a look at this,' he asked.

Leigh looked and then said, 'God, she obviously loved blue, as that's the only colour here, and she's arranged them all by shade, darkest to lightest.'

'Isn't that a bit unusual?'

'Possibly,' Leigh said hesitantly.

'Look again, look at what the clothes are.'

She looked again.

'Yes, I think I see what you mean. The clothes are only classified by their shade of blue. There are summer dresses, winter frocks and cardigans and they're all mixed up. Apparently only the shade of blue was important to her which is strange. Come to think of it all the walls are painted some shade of blue and the kitchen cabinets are blue too.'

45

'It's possible that Catherine could have been somewhere on the autistic spectrum, they call it Asperger's as well,' Mac said. 'We know that Catherine was quite directed and goal driven, her area of knowledge was specialised and that she wasn't all that good with people. It appears that she might have also had some sort of colour obsession which fits as well. People with Asperger's can suffer from a lack of empathy making it difficult for them to understand what other people are going through. It might have only been mild in her case and I believe that some of the symptoms lessen with age. We'll need to see her doctor at some point.'

'Oh, so she might not have actually been a cow but just someone who had limited social skills?'

'It's possible,' Mac conceded.

'Now I'm beginning to feel sorry for her,' Leigh said with a hint of sarcasm.

'To understand all is to forgive all, someone once said. Come on, let's go. We've still got lots to do today.'

As they walked back to the car Mac looked at his watch. It was nearly two o'clock.

'Let's find the nearest pub and get something to eat,' he said, 'with, perhaps, a side order of information.'

As they drove out Mac told Leigh to stop the car. He'd noticed that there was a metal post box attached to the garden wall. It was obviously there to save the postman a walk. He got the lockpicks out and had it open in seconds. A single white envelope lay within. He asked Leigh for an evidence bag and carefully placed the envelope within. It must have been hand delivered as there was no name or address on the front.

The nearest pub was no more than two hundred yards from Catherine's front door. It was called 'The Earl Lewin'. Mac stopped and smiled as he read the menu through the window.

'Why are you smiling?' Leigh asked.

'It's a gastro-pub and bloody expensive with it. Just the type of place someone like Catherine might frequent. Come on lunch is on me.'

The Second Poisoning

He took his time deciding on his second victim as he was somewhat spoilt for choice. However, the conviction soon grew on him that he should settle some outstanding family business next.

His wife had no close relations and neither did he, except for his aunt of course. Yes, his dear old auntie.

His father had died when he'd been very young so it had always been just him and his mother. She was now dead too and he had loved her dearly. However, he had realised from an early age that his mother had been weak. She'd never had a good opinion of herself and had always been too easily swayed by what other people said. And because of this, when he'd been young, he'd dreaded every one of his aunt's visits.

Her elder sister seemed to be all too aware of his mother's numerous faults and she was not backward at telling her about them. Her mothering skills she held in especial contempt. Every visit left his mother depressed for days afterwards. She would hold him and cry and apologise to him for being such a bad mother.

Even as a child he'd been strongly of the opinion that there was nothing wrong with his mother but it was her sister's skills as an aunt that were truly to be despised. She never forgot to forget his birthday although there was always a little something with his Aunt's name on it under the Christmas tree. When he was twelve, he'd discovered that it had actually been bought by his mother.

He hadn't seen much of his aunt since his mother's death but he thought now would be a good time to renew their acquaintance. There was a very good friend of his that he wanted her to meet.

He asked if he could pop around on the pretext of doing some family research. He brought her a little treat as thanks. His aunt was a great lover of sweet things and could never go past a pastry shop. He'd brought her favourite, a choux bun with chocolate on the top stuffed with cream and a liberal helping of Mr. T of course.

He watched her as she stuffed the pastry down her vile mouth with some satisfaction. Some cream had spilled on to the plate and she picked it up with her finger and then licked it all off.

That's it, auntie, he said to himself. Don't waste a bit.

The doctor rang him the day after. He said that his aunt was dying and, if he wanted to see her before she went, then he should come immediately. He was glad that she had the decency to die before he got there. There was no-one else there, just him and the doctor.

This would be the hardest part, convincing the doctor that the death was natural.

As it turned out the doctor made it easy for him. He told the doctor that his aunt had been ill for some time (which was a lie of course) but that she'd always been scared of seeking medical help (which was true). The doctor then asked a series of questions about chest pain and breathlessness. He congratulated the doctor on his skill in spotting every single one of her symptoms.

Only to be expected, the doctor supposed. She was in her sixties and she was quite overweight. With such a clear diagnosis the doctor felt that an autopsy wouldn't be needed.

The death certificate stated categorically that she had died of heart failure and that was that. He called the undertakers and, while he waited, he had a good look around his new house. Of course, as he was her only relation, everything would go to him. Besides the house there was a tidy sum in the bank and probably some insurance.

He tried to look sad as they took her body away and he thought he did quite well. However, as he went around the house locking doors and turning off lights he stopped and laughed out loud as he suddenly remembered something.

Before every visit by his aunt his mother would go to the baker's shop and buy a cake. They didn't have much money but his mother, afraid of her sister's bad opinion, always somehow managed to scrape together enough money to buy the best cake they had.

His aunt would survey the cake greedily and when offered a large slice she'd always say 'Oh you shouldn't have. One day these cakes will kill me.'

Chapter Six

Even though it was a weekday the pub was full and they had to wait for a table. Eventually a waiter led them towards the back of the room.

'Let's eat first and ask questions later. I always do it better on a full stomach,' Mac said.

Leigh chose the pan-fried salmon while Mac went for the cheapest dish on the menu, liver and bacon. It was really good and Mac made a mental note to bring Bridget here sometime. When the waiter returned with his credit card, Leigh showed her warrant card and Mac asked to see the manager.

A few minutes later a man dressed in a chef's outfit joined them and introduced himself.

'Hi, I'm Simon Gent. I own and run the pub.'

Mac was surprised as he was only in his late twenties if that. He spoke with an accent that Mac guessed would be from around the Bristol area. Leigh showed Simon her warrant card and introduced herself and Mac.

'You're quite busy for a lunchtime, what's it like in the evening?' Mac asked.

Mac was thinking of treating Bridget as it was her birthday in a couple of months.

'You'd need to book at least four or five weeks in advance, even longer for weekends. We even have people who turn up and wait just in case of cancellations,' Simon said with a hint of pride.

'Oh, I see. Anyway, we're investigating the death of Catherine Gascoigne who lived just down the road from here. I was also hoping that, as you were so near, she might have come here from time to time.'

'Oh, more often than that. She came twice a week as regularly as clockwork, except for the last week or two if I remember right. Same time, same table, the one over there in the corner by the window and she always ordered the same thing. She's dead you say?'

Mac nodded.

'Did she always come by herself?' Mac asked.

'I'm in the kitchen most of the time so I wouldn't know. You'd really need to speak to my head waiter Nico. I'll go and get him.'

He walked over and spoke to one of the waiters. Mac observed them both closely while they talked. A minute later Simon returned.

'This is my head waiter, Nico Panagos. He knows everyone who comes in here. Is it okay if I get back to the kitchen now?'

'Yes of course, thanks.'

Mac noticed the chef giving Leigh a lingering glance as he walked away. Leigh didn't seem to have noticed.

The waiter sat down. He was also in his late twenties but he was black haired, slim and very good looking. Mac thought he looked somewhat nervous which intrigued him.

'Mrs. Gascoigne, I knew she wasn't well and now you say she's dead?' he asked.

'Yes, she was found dead yesterday,' Mac replied. 'What can you tell me about her?'

He knew that the waiter had lost a valuable customer but the anguish Mac could see in his face hinted at there being more to it than that.

'Well, she came in every Tuesday and Friday. She always had the braised lamb with lentils on a Tuesday and the plaice, samphire and lemon butter on Fridays. She hated it when Simon changed the menu and she had to pick something new. She kept herself to herself and she always tipped well.'

'Did she generally eat by herself?' Mac asked.

'Almost always, although I did see her with someone, it must have been around four weeks ago I'd guess. We were really busy that night but I still noticed because it was so unusual.'

'Can you describe her companion?' Mac asked.

'An American woman, very elegantly dressed and in her mid-thirties I'd guess. She only had coffee.'

'Did you catch any of the conversation?'

'I didn't need to, Mrs. Gascoigne told me who the woman was later,' Nico said. 'She was a publisher who was commissioning a coffee table book on Jane Austen. Mrs. Gascoigne was really excited as she'd been asked to write a part of the book.'

'She didn't tell you what the woman's name was?'

'Yes, it was Gloria something...yes, Gloria Bridges.'

Mac was thoughtful for a short while.

'Is there anything else you can tell us?'

'No, as I said I just knew her from the restaurant.'

'Thank you, I think that will do.'

Outside Mac stood still for a moment. He was thinking about the waiter's reaction to the news that Catherine was dead.

'I'd be very surprised if Nico back there wasn't a bit more involved with Catherine than he's letting on.'

'What makes you think that?' Leigh asked.

'I watched him when his boss told him that we were investigating Catherine's death. I could see he was really shaken and when he said that he knew that Catherine was ill, I wondered how. Then, when he told us about the publisher and even knew her name, that made me even more suspicious.'

'Why was that?' Leigh asked.

'That restaurant was busy at two o'clock in the afternoon on a weekday and, according to its owner, it's heaving at night. As the head waiter I doubt that Nico ever has time to sit down with a guest and have any sort of conversation. From his reaction to the news of her death, and the fact that he knew that she'd been ill, I figure that their relationship might have been a little closer than that of waiter and customer.'

'Do you think that Nico might have had something to do with Catherine's murder then?'

'I'm not sure that I'd go as far as that but he certainly knows more than he's telling. I think we'll have to come back and speak Mr. Panagos again in due course. Anyway, what he told us about Catherine getting offered a book deal is interesting.'

'In what way?'

'Well, it pretty much rules out suicide I'd say,' Mac said as Leigh started the car. 'Let's try the sister-in-law next.'

Mac rang Mrs. Carnet's number to make sure she was in. She was not only in but seemed to be very much looking forward to seeing him.

They pulled up outside a house in Baldock that, while nice and still way beyond a policeman's salary, was on a more human scale. The door opened on the first ring of the bell and a squat woman in her sixties, grey haired and dressed all in black, opened the door. Mac introduced Leigh and himself and they were invited in without any further conversation.

'Would you like some tea?' the woman asked with a wide smile.

'Yes, please,' Mac replied.

He was feeling a little thirsty but it also gave him time to look around the room while Mrs. Carnet was gone. It was what his mother would have called the 'parlour', the one room in the house that was always kept in order and had the best furniture. Mac always knew a guest was special when they were ushered into the parlour rather than the kitchen.

It was nothing like his mother's parlour though. A large bow window had given that room light and it was the only place in their small house where a cat could have been swung. This room was gloomy and fusty and cluttered with furniture and ornaments.

The woman appeared with a little silver coloured trolley that had a teapot, three cups and saucers and a plate with a variety of biscuits on it.

'Mrs. Carnet, we're investigating the death of Mrs. Catherine Gascoigne and we'd like to ask you some questions, is that okay?' Mac said.

'Catherine's dead?'

Her smile widened considerably.

'You know, when I woke up this morning, I had a feeling that today was going to be a good day. How did she die?'

'She was poisoned,' Mac replied.

'Even better then. Well, as good as that news is, I was really hoping you'd come to ask me some questions about another murder.'

'Another murder?' Mac exclaimed with a puzzled expression.

'Yes, the murder of my brother. It was Catherine who killed him of course.'

'Let's get this straight. You suspect Catherine Gascoigne of killing her husband?'

'I don't suspect, I know. She and that doctor who wrote the death certificate were as thick as thieves. They did it together,' she stated as she poured tea into the cups. 'Milk, sugar?' she asked brightly.

Both Mac and Leigh asked for milk only.

'How long is it since your brother died?'

'It's nearly two years now.'

'So, tell me, what do you base your suspicions on?' Mac asked.

'Well, poor Richard was ill, anyone could see that.'

She silently mouthed the word 'Cancer'.

'The doctor at the hospital said he might have another three months, yet only two weeks later he was dead. Now, Catherine had known Dr. Lucey for years and he was always around the house. It wouldn't surprise me if they were lovers. After Richard's death, I went to the police and asked them to investigate but they said that they couldn't find any evidence that a crime had been committed and closed the case. Between you and me I don't think they even bothered looking.'

'Do you think the death of your brother might have anything to do with Catherine's death?' Mac asked.

The woman gave it some thought.

'Perhaps. What if the doctor bumped her off? What if Catherine, tortured by a guilty conscience, was about to confess and the doctor poisoned her to keep her mouth shut?'

Leigh noticed that Mac had a highly sceptical expression on his face as he asked, 'Mrs. Carnet, I take it that you're a lover of crime novels?'

'God yes, especially Agatha, but how did you know? Oh, of course you'd know, you're a detective, aren't you?' she said brightly.

'Okay, I promise I'll look into your brother's death but only if you answer my questions.'

'You've got a deal, fire away.'

'I take it that you and Catherine didn't get on. Why was that?' Mac asked.

'I must admit that I disliked her on sight. She definitely wasn't good enough for my Richard. She couldn't even have babies, or so Richard said. She wasn't a proper woman at all in my book. However, Richard liked her so I tried not to meddle. Then Richard got ill and she and that doctor were always fluttering around him, scared that I might have found out I guess.'

'Found out what?'

'That they were hurrying him along as it were.'

'And why would they do that?' Mac asked.

'To get him out of the way so they could get his money of course,' she said.

'How much was your brother worth?'

'More than eight and a half million pounds in cash if I remember right, then there was the house and some other properties. He was always good at business. Toby and I got a million each and the rest went to Catherine'

'What did he do?'

'He was a stockbroker in the City, a partner in a very successful firm.'

'And how was Catherine after your brother died?'

'I wouldn't know,' she replied with pursed lips. 'I only saw her once after the funeral when I bumped into her one day on the High Street. We just said hello really.'

'So, you haven't visited Catherine's house since the funeral?' Mac asked.

'No and I wouldn't go there even if I had been invited.'

'What about your other brother?' Mac asked.

'Toby? He came back to see Richard just before he died and then again for the funeral but he hasn't been back since as far as I know.'

Mac was silent for a moment.

'Have you any ideas who might have wanted to kill Catherine, apart from the doctor that is?'

She shrugged her shoulders.

'Half of that stupid Society she started up or so I've heard.'

'And what about you?' Mac asked pointedly.

'Oh, if I was going to kill her no-one would know about it, believe me. I know all the tricks of the trade from the books I've read but no I didn't kill Catherine. However, if I'm honest, I'm far from sad she's dead and more power to whoever did the dirty deed.'

Mac thought about this for a few moments then he asked, 'Tell me Mrs. Carnet, why are you wearing black? Has someone died?'

'Yes, my husband Raymond, poor dear,' Mrs. Carnet said with a very sad expression.

'I'm sorry to hear it. I take it that this happened recently?'

'Yes, it will be twelve years ago next month, it seems like yesterday though.'

Before he left, Mac asked her for the name of the doctor's surgery.

'Thank you, Mrs. Carnet. Please ring me at this number if you think of anything.'

Outside Mac and Leigh looked at each other.

'She's a bit strange!' Leigh exclaimed.

'You're right there,' Mac conceded.

'Did you believe her when she said she didn't do it?' Leigh asked.

'Well, she made it clear that she was more than happy that Catherine was dead and she did have a powerful motive but, if I'm being honest, I don't know. Her brother died a couple of years ago so, if it was her, then why wait that long? Come on, let's see this Dr. Lucey. We should just have time before we have to get back to the station.'

'Why the doctor?' Leigh asked.

'Firstly, because I'm wondering if there might be a nugget of truth in what Mrs. Carnet told us.'

'You think that this doctor and Catherine might really have killed her husband?'

Mac nodded.

'And secondly?' Leigh prompted.

'And secondly the doctor's surgery is on the way back to the station anyway.'

Leigh showed her warrant card and asked for the doctor at reception. Luckily, he was on duty and they got the message that he'd be free in ten minutes. Mac and Leigh sat down with the waiting patients. Just before the ten minutes were up Dr. Lucey appeared. He introduced himself and they followed him to his office. Mac noticed that they got a lot of sour looks as they went in. Their fellow waiters obviously had strong suspicions that they were queue jumping.

'So, how can I help the police?' the doctor asked brightly.

Mac looked him over. He was slim, in his late thirties, curly haired and was probably what some women might call 'cute'.

'We're investigating the death of Catherine Gascoigne and we've just had a very interesting conversation with her sister-in-law,' Mac said.

'I'll bet you did,' the doctor said with some feeling.

'Who told you that Catherine was dead?'

'I got a phone call from Penny Bathurst yesterday and another one about an hour ago,' the doctor replied. 'She told me that Catherine had been murdered. I still find it hard to believe that she's dead let alone that someone killed her.'

Mac thought the doctor still looked quite shaken.

'Was it you who treated Mrs. Gascoigne for a stomach problem?'

'Yes, she said that it had been causing her problems for a while. I gave her something for it and it seemed to do the trick. Was the stomach problem something to do with her death? Penny got a bit upset during the call and she didn't say exactly how Catherine died.'

'It was thallium poisoning,' Mac said.

'Thallium? That's bizarre!' the doctor exclaimed.

'In what way?'

'In every way, I mean I remember something about thallium during my training but I've never come across it as a doctor. God, the bad stomach, that's one of the symptoms, isn't it? If only I'd thought, if only I'd done some tests...'

'Don't blame yourself doctor,' Mac said. 'I believe that one of the things that made thallium such a popular poison years ago was that it's supposed to be very hard to diagnose and after all she only had a stomach upset.'

'I suppose you're right. I still wished I'd spotted it though,' the doctor said with a sad shake of his head.

'Is there anything that you can tell us that might help?' Mac asked.

59

'I wish I could. I had a lot of respect for Catherine. She was very supportive during a very dark time for me. After Richard died, we kind of drifted apart and, although we still saw each other from time to time, it was never quite the same.'

When he mentioned Richard Gascoigne's death Mac could see from his expression that it had hit him hard and it still hurt. From what the doctor said it would seem that it was Richard Gascoigne who had been the more important to him in some way.

'Tell me, what was your relationship with Richard Gascoigne?' Mac asked.

'Relationship, what do you mean?' the doctor said too quickly.

Mac didn't reply, he just sat there and looked keenly at the doctor's face. The doctor stood up and paced up and down for a few seconds. From his expression Mac knew he'd come to some sort of a decision. He sat down again.

'My relationship with Richard? It's something that I've been denying for years now, mostly at Richard's request, but I've had enough of that. I'm not going to deny Richard again. Richard and I were lovers, I loved him with all my heart.'

'Doctor, did you kill Richard Gascoigne?'

The doctor hesitated for a moment then he looked levelly at Mac.

'Yes, I did,' he said, 'I gave Richard a lethal dose of morphine. I killed him.'

Chapter Seven

Mac glanced over to see an expression of astonishment on Leigh's face. He carried on questioning the doctor.

'Dr. Lucey, why did you kill Richard Gascoigne?'

'I killed him because I loved him,' the doctor replied. 'His prognosis was as bad as it could be. There was a high probability that he might last for months and an even higher probability that the pain would get worse, much worse. Poor Richard couldn't bear it as it was and it was breaking all our hearts to see him like that.'

'Whose hearts?'

'Catherine's, Toby's and mine of course.'

'So, Catherine and Toby knew all about this?' Mac asked.

'Yes, of course. Catherine and I had discussed it for weeks before we spoke about it to Toby over the phone. He'd always been close to Richard so we thought that he should be consulted too. He flew over straight away and we took him through every possibility we could think of. In the end he agreed that killing Richard was the best thing that we could do for him.'

'What about Richard himself?' Mac asked.

'It was him begging us to end his misery that started us thinking about it in the first place. We would never have done anything without him being a totally willing party.'

'Why didn't you involve his sister?'

The doctor laughed.

'You've met her, would you?'

Mac had to admit that the doctor had a point.

'Why you though?' Mac asked. 'Why didn't Catherine or Toby give him the lethal dose?'

'It was Richard's request, he said it would be better. He said that both of them would benefit from his will whereas I would get nothing. He joked that the real reason was that they'd probably break the needle or something.'

'Did you mind not being mentioned in the will?'

The doctor shook his head.

'No, I have money of my own and even at the end Richard didn't want people to know about us. I could only respect his wishes.'

'Were there any last words?' Mac asked.

'Yes,' the doctor said softly as tears started to fall down his cheeks. 'Yes, there were. As I injected him, he whispered in my ear. He said the real reason why he wanted me to give him the injection was because he loved me the most.'

He gave Mac an intensely sad look then broke down and started sobbing uncontrollably. Leigh looked over at Mac as though she thought they should do something. Mac sat still and gave the situation some thought while he waited for the doctor to recover his composure.

'Are you okay to carry on?' Mac asked gently a few minutes later.

The doctor nodded.

'How would you describe Catherine, I mean from a medical point of view?'

The doctor dried his eyes with a tissue.

'What do you mean?'

'Did she have Asperger's? Was she on the autistic spectrum?'

'I'm no expert but I did consult someone once about Catherine. I was at a conference a few years back and one of the seminars was about autism. Afterwards I spoke to one of the specialists and described her behaviours as truthfully as I could.'

'And what was the outcome?' Mac asked.

'Of course, the specialist couldn't be absolutely sure without actually seeing her but he was fairly certain she was somewhere on the autistic spectrum. The way she clung on to old friends, kept to a strict routine and hated

62

any change were all signs. Then there was the fact that she clearly had problems reading other people's reactions to what she said or did. However, it was her obsession with colour that interested him most.'

'Yes, we saw that when we looked in her wardrobe,' Mac said.

'She would only ever wear blue. For some reason she was obsessed with the colour. That's why Penny took over responsibility for the balls, apparently poor Catherine's idea of colours for the decor of the first ball looked quite strange.'

'Did this specialist say anything else?'

'Only that, in his opinion, life for people like Catherine could be like living in a constant storm. Their life rafts, the familiar things they cling to and their routines, were often the only things that stopped them from going under.'

Mac looked at his watch.

'Thanks for that Doctor. Well, we best get going.'

Dr. Lucey stood up.

'Yes, yes of course. I'll ring through and cancel my appointments for the rest of the day.'

'Now, why would you do that?' Mac asked, looking genuinely puzzled.

The doctor returned his puzzled look.

'I thought that you'd want me to come to the station with you. After all I've just admitted that I killed someone.'

'If we banged up every doctor who did what you've done the NHS queues would double overnight. I suffer from chronic pain myself, not as nearly bad as Richard's was, thank God. Even so, if the day ever comes that I can really no longer cope it's my hope that I'll find a doctor as sympathetic as you. Just carry on being the best doctor you can, that's your sentence as far as I'm concerned.'

The doctor looked both relieved and grateful.

'Thank you, Mr. Maguire, I'll do my best.'

'Again, I have to ask how you knew?' Leigh asked as they walked out of the surgery.

'Simply the look on his face when he talked about Richard. I've seen that same look many times before.'

'Where?'

'I see it most days when I look in the mirror,' Mac replied. 'Losing someone you were really close to leaves a kind of imprint, a haunted look on the face. When I saw that look, and coupled it with the fact that Richard died a lot sooner than predicted, it was easy really. Obviously, hearing about Catherine's death has brought it all back to him.'

'So, Catherine really did kill her husband, her gay husband come to that. Do you think that she ever really cared about Richard?'

'I think that she cared alright, in fact I think that she cared very much. I think that she probably loved Richard very much in her own way.'

'How could you possibly know that?' Leigh asked.

'The bedroom, it was a shrine. Left exactly as it was when Richard was still alive yet still maintained and cleaned. If Richard's sister or brother had ever visited the house then I might have reached the conclusion that it might have been just for show. However, Catherine could have removed all trace of him from the house or just locked the room and forgot about it if she'd wanted to, but she didn't. I think she probably loved him very much.'

Leigh sighed.

'You're right, people are complicated.'

'You don't need to have sex with people to love them,' Mac said. 'Catherine had created a fiction with Richard, a fiction that suited them both. I suppose they were a bit old fashioned really, keeping up appearances and all that. Anyway, being married meant that Richard could have his gay liaisons and Catherine didn't have to deal with the daily interactions of a real relationship, interactions that she wouldn't have been able to understand or cope with. She didn't have to worry about that with Richard.'

'Yes, I suppose you can't live with someone every day without becoming attached to them in some way.'

'Have you ever been involved in a mercy killing case yourself?' Mac asked.

Leigh shook her head.

'I've been involved in quite a few over the years and not one of them has ever led to a jail sentence,' Mac said. 'The usual outcome is lots of upset for everyone concerned and lots of time wasted for us. By the way are you okay with what I said to the doctor back there?'

'Yes, I think so,' she replied with some hesitation.

Mac frowned.

'I'm sorry, perhaps I should have asked you first before letting the doctor off the hook. When I was in the force, I'd worked with my sergeant for so long that I never had to ask him anything. If you have any second thoughts about it let me know.'

Leigh promised that she would.

'Come on,' Mac said, 'let's get back to the station and see what Andy's turned up.'

Leigh gave Mac a look as they walked back to the car. She'd wondered at being lumbered with an old duffer with a crutch on her first day. It had crossed her mind that it might have been some sort of elaborate prank. She didn't think that now. She decided that she needed to find out more about her new partner.

Back at the station Mac started summarising everything they'd found out on a white board while they waited for Andy and Toni to turn up.

'Not bad for less than a day's work,' Leigh commented as he wrote.

'You're right. We've discovered quite a bit about Catherine, loved by a few and disliked by many. I wonder how much her Asperger's was really to blame for the latter. I suppose it's quite possible for someone to have Asperger's and still be bit of a cow at the same time.'

'Sorry we're a bit late,' Andy said as he and Toni walked in. 'The traffic was awful.'

He took off his coat and read what was on the white board.

'You've been busy then. By the way Toby Gascoigne got in contact with us from Canada. He was obviously upset at the news but he couldn't really add anything to what we already know. However, as he's executor of Catherine Gascoigne's will, he did tell us who she left all her money to, all thirteen million pounds or so of it.'

Mac and Leigh leant forward expectantly.

'It's gone to charity unfortunately, every penny of it,' Andy said with a frown. 'So, we can probably rule that out as a motive. Anyway, take us through what you've found out so far.'

Mac handed over the evidence bags containing the stone, the key and the envelope and then walked Andy and Toni through each interview. He didn't mention anything about Dr. Lucey or Richard Gascoigne's death.

'That kind of fits with what we've found,' Andy said. 'We went to the university first and interviewed her line manager and some of her colleagues. She'd worked in the English department for over ten years. As part of her duties she'd normally have to do so many lectures a year and take on a set of students for one to one tuition. However, once they realised that, in her manager's words, 'Her people skills were virtually zero', she was allocated different work. They got her working on setting up the courses, auditing and also marking all the tests and exams. Her manager said she was by far the most consistent marker she'd ever come across and pretty much set the benchmark across all of their English courses. 'Invaluable' was the word she used.

However, she didn't interact with her colleagues very much. Most days she'd come into the office and just get on with her work, sometimes without saying a word to anyone all day.'

'It was probably her ideal job in a way,' Mac said.

'Well, she certainly wasn't disliked at the University as I far as I could see and I doubt anyone there knew her well enough to want to kill her anyway.'

Andy picked up the evidence bag and looked at the key.

'Why do people make it so bloody easy to get into their houses? Same story I'm hearing time after time with these burglaries, doors left unlocked, keys hidden under mats and in plant pots, alarm codes like 1-2-3-4 then some of them think they've been clever just because they've changed it to 4-3-2-1.'

Andy stopped seeing the expression on Mac's face.

'No!'

'All too unfortunately, yes,' Mac replied. 'Apparently, Catherine told one of the Society's members, a woman called Molly Etherington, what the code was and where the key was hidden. God knows how many other people Molly might have told. What about the Settlement? Did you find out anything there?'

'Well, her course was quite popular,' Andy replied. 'Although her teaching style was basically just talking at people and she didn't always handle interruptions all that well, people said they still liked the course because she really knew her stuff. One of the other tutors also said that, when she was asked something she didn't know, she always found out and would come back with an answer if it was at all possible. So, what do you think, should we concentrate on the Janeites for now?' Andy asked

'Yes, in my opinion they're definitely our best bet,' Mac replied. 'Not forgetting the ex-Janeites, so we'll need to talk to Anne Holding's little group as well. By the way, is there any news about Mrs. Parker's computer yet?'

'Why? Do you think there might be something important on there?' Andy asked.

'I'm fairly sure that there's something on there that Mrs. Parker didn't want us to see. It might not be relevant to the case but you never know.'

'I'll check my emails.'

While Andy was on his computer Toni organised some coffees.

While they were gone Leigh turned to Mac.

'I've decided that I'm absolutely okay about Dr. Lucey and Richard Gascoigne. I just needed to give it some thought.'

'Thanks Leigh. I think that the poor doctor's probably gone through quite enough as it is without being hauled up in front of a judge and jury.'

Leigh didn't say anything. She looked at Mac and found that she couldn't make him out. He was a strange one for sure and unlike any policeman she'd ever met.

'So, tell me what did you think of today?' Mac asked.

'It's been interesting,' she replied. 'It's like starting with just an outline sketch of a person and we're gradually filling in the details, finding out a little bit at a time about what made them tick.'

'That's not a bad way of looking at it,' Mac said. 'So, if it's okay, can you come and pick me up fairly early tomorrow? Amanda usually walks her dog around nine and I'd like to catch her before she goes out. I'd like to see where the squirrel died and after that we might have a word with the vet she took it to before we start on the other interviews.'

'That's okay with me,' Leigh said with a little shrug of the shoulders.

Toni had just come back with the coffees when Andy entered the room looking somewhat perplexed.

'Any news on the hard drive yet?' Mac asked.

'I should say so,' Andy replied. 'They've sent me all the current and deleted files related to the membership of the Society but there's more. The computer expert I spoke to said that they came across some highly encrypted files which had originally been deleted a year or so ago. Of course, they had no problem resurrecting them and they're trying to break the encryption now. I doubt that it has much to do with our case but I suppose it'll keep them happy for a while. Okay, any suggestions about tomorrow?'

'I'd like to take Anne Holding's group if that's okay,' Mac said. 'But, in case we forget, there's been another death in this case. I'll try to interview Amanda and the vet she brought the squirrel to as well.'

'That would be good. If an animal can get at such a deadly poison then others might too,' Andy replied. 'We'll go and see this Tanya Stokes and go through the list of members with her. Hopefully she'll be able to identify some possibilities.'

'Oh, in case I forget, is there any chance that you can dig up the file on Philippa Hatch?' Mac asked.

'The girl who committed suicide? Sure.'

'She lived in Hitchin and she died about a year ago. It's probably nothing but you never know.'

Andy smiled.

'In my experience it's rarely 'nothing' if you're interested in it. It will be no problem. I'll send a request to records before I go,' Andy said as he stood up. 'Okay that's it for today then. We'll catch up at the same time tomorrow if that's alright.'

Outside the station Mac asked, 'What are you doing now?'

'Going home I suppose,' Leigh replied, 'only it doesn't feel much like that yet. Anyway, I don't know anyone here and I've still got some boxes to unpack...'

'You could come with me if you like,' Mac offered. 'I'm going to meet my friend for a drink.'

He thought that, with her being new to Letchworth, she might be grateful for a little company. He was quite surprised when her defences slammed up and she backed off a step.

'No, thanks but no. After all those boxes won't unpack themselves. See you tomorrow.'

She then scurried off.

Mac was thoughtful as he made his way to the Magnets. As he walked by the pub Tim waved at him through the plate glass window. He'd managed to get their favourite table in the corner, number thirteen, underneath the photographs of George Bernard Shaw.

Mac made himself comfortable while Tim got a round in. When Tim returned with the drinks Mac raised his glass to the photo of the great man before taking a gulp.

'So, what have you been up to today?' Tim asked.

Mac told him of the circumstances around the two poisonings.

'And was it only yesterday that you were saying that a few quiet days might not be a bad thing after your little trip to Birmingham?' Tim joshed. 'So, what do you think?'

'It's too early to tell but I can't shake this feeling that the poisonings are somehow connected to the suicide, although where the squirrel fits in, God knows. I might be wrong though. Miss Hatch apparently had no relatives or close friends so there's no-one with sufficient motive to seek revenge. Still tomorrow's another day and you never know what we might discover.'

They both invested in a foot-long hot dog and while they ate Mac told his friend of his adventures in his home town. He'd even managed to see an Aston Villa match and he described the game in detail, trying not to dwell too long on the eighty ninth minute own goal that lost them the game.

Later, as he made himself a coffee before going to bed, he thought through the case again. He had no clear idea of where it was going and of the inevitable surprises that he knew must be in store but he didn't care. He smiled to himself. He was working on a real case again and that was more than enough.

Chapter Eight

Tuesday

'It was just there, on the ground by the bird feeder,' Amanda said pointing with her finger.

The bird feeder was roughly in the same position as the one he had in his own back garden, being about fifteen feet straight in front of the kitchen window.

'I take it you like watching the birds as you wash up,' Mac said.

'And while I'm cooking. I love the Robins and the Coal Tits and we even get some Corn Buntings, believe it or not. They come in a little flock and they're quite funny as they form a sort of queue to feed.'

'What about squirrels?' Mac asked.

'Yes, there used to be two black ones and I sometimes put peanuts out for them,' Amanda said. 'I liked them as much as the birds if I'm honest, there's something quite cheeky about them.'

'And it was one of those that you found dead?' Mac asked.

'Well, if I'm honest I can't be sure if it's the same squirrel but it looked the same. The vet said that it was an adult male.'

'You said that the squirrel was still alive when you found it?' Mac asked.

Amanda looked upset just thinking about it.

'Yes, I saw the poor little thing trying to get up to the feeder but it looked like it was drunk or something. Then it fell to the ground and lay there twitching. I just didn't know what to do.'

'Well, as it turned out, I think that you did exactly the right thing,' Mac said.

He got the name of the vet from her. The practice was on Norton Way just a short drive from Amanda's house.

It had only just gone nine as Mac and Leigh pulled into the car park. Even this early in the day the waiting room was full of glum faced people clutching a variety of boxes and dogs on leads. Mac wouldn't have thought it possible but the dogs looked even more miserable than their owners. Luckily Mr. Notts, a young man dressed in a white lab coat with a red bow tie, was able to see them immediately.

'I've only ever had one case of squirrel poisoning before and that was the squirrel's own fault really. It had gotten into a workshop and helped itself from an open tin of welding flux. Otherwise it's mostly injuries from air guns I'm afraid.'

'Have you ever come across a case of thallium poisoning in any animal before?' Mac asked.

The vet shook his head.

'I asked one of my older colleagues and he said that many years ago they used to get lots of them. People used to leave it out as a rat poison and other animals used to pick it up.'

Mac gave this some thought.

'Squirrels are rodents too, aren't they?'

'Absolutely, oh, I think I see what you're getting at,' the vet said. 'I suppose if there was any rat poison left lying around then they might find it as attractive as the rats did.'

'So, if there were still some old tins or packets of rat poison knocking about then you think it's possible that our squirrel might have helped himself to some?' Mac asked.

'Yes, it's not unlikely,' the vet replied. 'We've just had a period of very cold weather and I suppose food has been scarce. As well as that, squirrels sometimes nest in sheds or outhouses and that's where most people would store a poison like that.'

Mac thought for a moment.

'How far might our squirrel have come? It's possible that he was a regular visitor.'

'Well the males can sometimes go quite a distance, especially during the mating season. However, I'd guess that, if you drew a circle of around a half a kilometre from where you found it, then you wouldn't be too far out. If it was a regular visitor though, it's highly likely to have been much closer than that.'

As they walked back to the car Mac said, 'Remind me to print off a map when we get the chance. As the vet said it's possible that whoever killed Catherine Gascoigne was keeping the poison in a shed or outhouse and that's how the squirrel met its end. We need to check every Janeite's and ex-Janeite's address and see if any of them live within half a kilometre of Amanda's house.'

'So, where to now?' Leigh asked.

Mac looked at her closely. There was definitely something a little different about her manner today.

'Let's go back to the library. We need to see Anne Holding again.'

Unlike the previous visit Anne showed no nervousness and gave Mac a big smile when she caught sight of him. She once again led them to kitchen and this time she made coffee for them all.

'You know, I still can't believe that Catherine's dead,' Anne said. 'I thought that I'd be quite happy about it but I find that I'm exactly the opposite. Someone killed her and it might be someone I know. That's not a very comforting thought.'

Mac was interested in seeing her reaction so he told her what the doctor had told him about Catherine and the likelihood she was on the Autistic spectrum.

Anne looked quite shocked and didn't say anything for a while.

'You know it makes absolute sense when I think about it now. I know someone who's an Aspie, he has Asperger's and that's what he calls himself, and I suppose that I should have guessed. It really explains a lot.'

'I'll need the name of everyone who attends your group and addresses too if possible,' Mac asked.

'It's quite an informal meeting so we don't have membership records or anything,' Anne said. 'We contact each other by email, I only know where Diane and Molly live.'

'Is that Molly Etherington?' Mac asked, beginning to feel a little excited.

'Yes, that's right, she used to be a member of the Society but she left,' Anne replied.

'Why was that?'

'It had something to do with the decorations for one of the balls or so I was told. They had to be temporarily stored somewhere and Catherine said that she had some room in her house. She said that she'd given Molly strict instructions where to put them but somehow Molly had still managed to put them in the wrong place. Well, Catherine tore a strip off Molly in front of everyone and poor Molly really took it to heart. She never went to another meeting again. Mind you, knowing now that Catherine had Asperger's, I can sort of understand why she might have been so angry. Any mess can be quite painful for them. You don't think it could possibly be Molly who killed Catherine though, do you?'

'We just need to check,' Mac replied in a neutral voice.

Anne wrote down the names of the other women who attended the meetings. She also included Diane's and Molly's addresses.

'That story you told me about Catherine and Philippa Hatch at the ball, who else have you told that to?'

'Well, I told the police not long after she killed herself,' Anne said. 'Other than that, I think I've only mentioned it once. It sort of popped out once when we were talking about Catherine at one of our meetings. We were at Diane's and she's always quite liberal with the wine.'

Noticing some computers, Mac asked, 'Anne, you couldn't do me a favour could you?'

She printed off a map and even drew a circle to scale. Mac thanked her and left.

Outside Mac handed Leigh the map.

'Look where Molly lives,' he said.

'It's in the next street to Amanda's!' Leigh said excitedly. 'She also had access to the house and a good motive for killing Catherine.'

'Yes, it's getting interesting, isn't it?'

Before they drove off Mac contacted the station and gave the names that he'd gotten from Anne to one of the detectives. He said he'd ring back as soon as he had their addresses.

Luckily Molly was at home. Leigh flashed her warrant card. She didn't seem at all surprised.

'I thought that I might be getting a visit from the police before long,' she said as she let them in.

'Why's that?' Mac asked.

'I got a phone call a short while ago from one of the members of the Society who I'm still friendly with. She told me that Catherine had been murdered and it's common knowledge that she and I had fallen out.'

She didn't seem unduly upset about the fact. Molly Etherington was a slim, bird like woman in her fifties. They sat down in the only bit of free space in the living room. The rest of the room was taken up with piles of magazines and a long clothes rack that was jammed with an assortment of dresses and cardigans. Mac noticed that Molly couldn't seem to keep her hands still. She kept rearranging the coasters on the coffee table as she spoke to Mac. He wondered if she might really have something to be nervous about.

'Why did you and Catherine fall out?' he asked.

'I'm sure you'll have already heard the story from Anne.'

'I'd like to hear it from you if you don't mind,' Mac insisted.

'Very well then. It all started because we needed somewhere to store some decorative swags for the ball.'

On seeing Leigh's look of incomprehension Molly explained.

'They're a long sort of garland I suppose, made up of green branches and the like, and decorated with pine cones and berries and woodland bits and bobs. It was the ball at the Crown from Emma so we thought it might be just the type of thing that they'd have used to decorate the ballroom. Ours were all fake of course, but they looked real enough. We also had some bolts of fabric that we were going to drape about the place and it was all a bit bulky. I volunteered to pick it all up from the suppliers as I drive an old Volvo and, with the back seats down, you can fit quite a bit inside. Catherine told me where to find the key to her house and the code for the burglar alarm and I put it all where she'd told me to put it, in the living room. I thought it was a bit too nice to be used for storing decorations but, knowing what she's like, I just did as I was told.'

Molly paused and slowly shook her head.

'We had a meeting the next night and Catherine totally lost it. What was it she said? Yes, she said that I was at best an idiot and at worst malicious. Well I couldn't have that, could I? So, I told her where to stick her Society and walked out.'

'I take it that you never went back?' Mac asked.

'No and I suppose that, if I'm being totally honest, there was another reason for that. It turned out that Catherine had been right. One of the other members told me afterwards that she'd overheard the conversation and that Catherine had definitely told me that the decorations should be put in the dining room at the back of the house and that she'd actually repeated it several times. I must have gotten mixed up I suppose and I put them in the living room instead. I do get mixed up sometimes but there was still no reason to talk to me like that, was there?'

Mac pictured Catherine's living room in his head, spotless and everything precisely in its place, and he could almost understand why Catherine might have lost her temper.

Mac decided to try the blunt approach and see what happened.

'Did you kill Catherine Gascoigne?'

Molly didn't look fazed in the slightest.

'No, although I must admit I've thought about it more than once. Running her over with the old Volvo would have been my way of doing it though and perhaps backing over her once or twice just to make sure.'

'Do you mind if we look around?' Mac asked.

For the first time Molly looked concerned.

'Why, what are you looking for?'

'Nothing in particular. Can we?'

She gave this some thought.

'I suppose,' she eventually said with some reluctance.

Her reluctance increased Mac's interest.

'Do you have a shed or an outhouse?' Mac asked.

Molly looked puzzled.

'Yes, but why would you want to look at that?'

'Just humour me,' Mac replied.

The shed was brick built and quite substantial. Molly opened the door and the musty smell of rodents hit his nostrils.

'Well, something's been living in here,' Mac said.

'I've noticed field mice nesting in here before,' Molly volunteered. 'I don't really mind them so long as they're gone by the time that I need to get the mower out to cut the grass.'

Mac's eye was caught by a red package that stood on a shelf at about head height. It was red and had a drawing of a rat that was lying on its back.

'What's that?' Mac asked.

'I'm not sure,' Molly replied.

She moved the lawn mower to get a closer look.

'It's rat poison, I think,' she said as she raised her hand to touch it.

'Don't touch it!' Mac said forcefully as her hand went towards the poison. 'Look!'

He pointed to the corner of the packet which had been gnawed away. Some of the poison had leaked and tiny paw prints could be seen.

Molly looked around at Mac with a shocked expression on her face.

'You don't think...you couldn't...I mean that must have been there for years. I didn't even know it was there.'

Mac turned to Leigh and whispered, 'I'm phoning Andy. Can you get her back in the living room and don't let her out of your sight until you're relieved.'

'Do you think that she might be the murderer?' Leigh whispered back.

'If I'm honest, I'm not sure, but it looks like she might have had the means to carry out the murder as well as a motive. I can't take the chance.'

He rang Andy Reid and told him what he'd found. Andy said that he'd be there in fifteen minutes and that he'd also arrange for a forensics team to visit as soon as possible. He asked Mac if he could stay where he was until they arrived. Mac decided to have a look around the rest of the house while he waited.

He found it difficult to make his way around as every room was so full of junk, even the upstairs bathroom had stacks of old newspapers in one corner. However, there was one room upstairs that was locked. Mac got out his lock picks and had the door open in seconds. Even he was surprised at what the room contained.

No wonder she didn't want us looking around, Mac thought. He went back downstairs and Molly gave him a questioning look.

'I've looked in all the rooms upstairs Molly,' he said, stressing the word 'all'.

She said nothing. After a few seconds she nodded her head and the nervousness was replaced by a look of resignation. He knew then that his guess had been right.

A few minutes later the bell rang and Mac ushered Andy and Toni in. He gestured at them to follow him outside. He showed them the rat poison.

'Do you think she did it then?' Andy asked.

Mac shook his head.

'No, I don't think it's her. She seemed genuinely surprised when I found the rat poison and the tracks look a bit small for a squirrel. She obviously resented Catherine greatly but, that being the case, why wait for a year before killing her?'

Andy went and took a look.

'I see what you mean about the tracks. We'll get forensics to take a look anyway. So, you think she may be innocent?'

'Of murder at least.'

'What do you mean?' Andy looked intrigued. 'You think she's guilty of something else, don't you?'

'Follow me and I'll show you,' Mac said.

As they trooped through the living room on their way upstairs Molly watched them go by with an expression that was half-smile, half-grimace.

'Here,' Mac said, pointing to the door.

Andy opened the door and looked inside.

'Good God!' he exclaimed and then motioned for Toni to follow him inside.

Mac stayed in the hallway, there was barely room for two inside the door.

'What's she doing, starting up her own shop up or something?' Toni said with some surprise.

'Tell me what you see,' Mac asked.

'There are toys and children's clothes, all boys' from what I can see. There are socks, trousers, shirts, underwear and yet more kid's toys, stacked right up to the ceiling. Boxes and boxes of them and most of them still in their original packaging. Does she have any children?' Toni asked.

'There's none living with her now but I'll bet she had one once,' Mac replied with certainty.

'You think that she's a shoplifter, don't you?' Andy asked.

'Yes, I'd bet on it and a good one too if she's managed to steal all that without getting caught.'

'But why? It doesn't look as if she's even opened any of this stuff,' Toni asked.

'Some people steal for the thrill of it but it can also be a cry for help,' Mac replied. 'In my time I've come across quite a few shoplifters who were quite relieved to get caught, it brought whatever personal crisis they were going through to a head.'

'Let's get her down the station then,' Andy said. 'Mac, would you mind hanging around until the forensics team arrives? I'll send a uniform down as soon as I can to keep them company.'

'No problem. Do me a favour though, I asked for some addresses earlier, do you think he could bring them with him?'

'I'll make sure he does,' Andy said. 'I'll see you later for the debrief.'

Molly didn't seem surprised when Andy asked her to accompany him to the station, if anything her expression was one nearer relief. She got her coat on, gave Mac a pale smile and meekly followed the two policemen out.

'Does Andy really think she murdered Catherine?' Leigh asked.

'No, she's not being arrested for that. We found an Ali Baba's cave of stuff upstairs, almost certainly stolen.'

'You mean Molly's a shoplifter?'

'Yes, but she didn't steal for herself, she only stole children's clothes and toys, all unopened,' Mac said. 'I'd really like to know why though.'

He rang Amanda and asked her if Molly had ever had any children. She told him that she had once talked about a son. He was living in Australia now and, apparently, she hadn't seen him for quite some time.

When he'd finished speaking to Amanda, he told Leigh the news.

'I thought she might have had a child who died but Australia? Well, that's a kind of bereavement too, I suppose.'

'So, what do we do now?' Leigh asked.

'We sit and wait for forensics to show up.'

Mac sat down and made himself comfortable.

'Tell me do people still surprise you?' Leigh asked.

Mac looked her with interest.

'Why do you ask?'

Her shoulders slumped.

'Well, I looked you up on Google last night. I was curious but, if I'm honest, I wasn't expecting to find anything.'

'And did you?'

Leigh nodded.

'Wikipedia has quite a bit on you. You know, I wondered why DI Reid put me with you. I figured out that you were an ex-policeman but I wouldn't have guessed that you once headed the Met's Murder Squad. I looked up some of your cases too.'

'And did you find them interesting?' Mac asked.

She nodded.

'Anyway,' he continued, 'you were asking if people still surprised me and I'd have to say yes, all the time. When you take a big step back the patterns of behaviour can be near enough the same but I find that the texture

82

of each case is always different. I never find people boring.'

'I've noticed that, when you ask a question, you're always looking quite hard at how they react as well as listening to what they say,' Leigh said.

'Body language is very hard to disguise, although I've known one or two who could do it, but generally I must admit that I trust someone's reaction more than what they say. Words can be very slippery, can't they?'

'So, tell me, what did you notice about Molly then?' Leigh asked.

'Her reaction when I asked if we could have a look around was quite revealing,' he replied. 'Before that I couldn't quite make out if she was nervous about us being here or if she was just one of those people who fidget all the time. Then there was the rat poison. I could see that she was really surprised at it being there at all and, not only that, if I hadn't stopped her, I'm sure that she'd have touched it. If she had killed Catherine with that poison, she'd know how deadly it is and wouldn't have wanted to get so close to it. So, if I'm honest, I didn't fancy her for the murder but I was certain that she was hiding something. Then, when I looked in the locked room, I knew that she had something to be nervous about.'

Mac heard some sounds from the front of the house and opened the door. A big van was parked half on the pavement and two men were getting into white plastic all-in-ones. When they'd dressed one of the men approached Mac as he pulled his gloves on while the other was taping the front fence - 'Crime Scene – Do not enter.'

'Mr. Maguire, I take it?' he said.

Mac noticed that forensics people never shook hands much even when they weren't gloved up.

'Yes, that's me.'

'I'm Bob Yeardley, I'd be grateful if you could show me what you've found.'

Bob went back to the van and pulled out what looked like a very large black toolbox. It was his forensics kit. Mac led him through the house and showed him the rat poison in the shed. Bob opened up his box and got a large clear plastic evidence bag from it. He carefully picked up the packet of rat poison and placed it in the bag and sealed it. He held it up and looked at the back of the packet.

'Your case involves thallium doesn't it?' Bob asked.

'That's right.'

'Well, this isn't the source then. This poison is Warfarin based.'

He placed the bag carefully in his box.

'Is there anything else that I should be looking at?' Bob asked.

Mac led him to the upstairs room. Leigh followed them. He could see that, even though Leigh knew what was in the room, she was still surprised at just how much of it there was.

'I take it that you think that all of this is stolen?' Bob asked.

'Hopefully you'll be able to confirm that for us,' Mac replied. 'It would be nice if we could trace some of the more recent items back to the shops they were lifted from.'

'I've never seen anything quite like this before,' Bob said. 'All kid's stuff and look at that over there, an old Gameboy still in its original packaging. I used to play one of those when I was a kid.'

'It looks like she's been doing it for quite a while then.'

'Well, we've got our work cut out alright.'

'I'll let you get on with it then,' Mac said.

'Can you tell my partner to join me up here?' Bob asked with a sigh.

As he was doing so a police car pulled up. A uniformed policeman got out.

'Are you Mr. Maguire?' he asked.

'Yes, that's me,' Mac confirmed.

'DI Reid said that I should give you this.'

He handed Mac a sheet of paper. Mac thanked him and headed for the car. He felt a sharp stab of pain as he bent down to get into the car and, once seated, he pretended to study the sheet of paper until it went away. When he could think again, he pulled out the map.

'Unfortunately, none of these addresses are within a half kilometre of Amanda's house.'

He handed the paper to Leigh.

'So, where to first?' she asked.

'I suggest that we visit Catherine Mathers first and then Peggy Corning. We'll leave the other two until later. So, we need to head out towards Baldock and then over to the other side of the golf club.'

'Do you think it might be an idea for you to have a rest after that?' Leigh asked with some concern. 'I could see you were in a bit of pain as you got into the car.'

'Well noticed,' Mac replied. 'Yes, I suppose a lie down for an hour or so won't hurt.'

He glanced over at Leigh as they drove away. He was beginning to think that they might get on.

Catherine Mathers lived in a small modern estate about halfway between Letchworth and Baldock. Mac's knock on the door was answered by a plump grey-haired woman.

Leigh held up her warrant card.

Mac introduced Leigh and then started to introduce himself.

She put her glasses on and peered at Mac as he spoke. He was just about to explain why they were there when Mrs. Mathers interrupted him.

'Yes, of course you are. How exciting! I take it you're here about Catherine?'

She ushered them both inside.

Although both women lived alone this house was the exact opposite of Molly Etherington's being spacious and comfortable looking. Mac thought it was the first house he'd seen in this investigation that he might actually consider living in.

'Tea or coffee?' she asked.

'Coffee please, Mrs. Mathers,' Mac replied.

'Oh, please call me Kay. And you dear?' she asked turning to Leigh.

'Can I just have a glass of water?' Leigh asked.

'Of course, coming up.'

She disappeared into the kitchen.

'I never turn down a cup of coffee or tea when offered,' Mac stated. In a lower voice he continued, 'Water's too quick. Tea or coffee always gives you the chance for a sneaky look around.'

He looked first at the pictures on the mantelpiece. A slightly younger Kay Mathers standing by a sea wall with a man in his fifties, the dead husband Mac surmised. Beside that there was another photo with an even younger Kay standing in a garden with a small boy and even smaller girl. From what she was wearing, Mac guessed it was taken sometime in the seventies.

He glanced over towards the picture window underneath which a small desk was situated. On the desk there was an open laptop and a wooden book stand that had a magazine on it. On the wall next to the desk there were two cork boards that had cut-out newspaper and magazine articles pinned to them. He went over and had a look. They were all about crime, murders mostly.

'Bloody hell!' Leigh heard Mac exclaim softly.

'What is it?' she asked.

She came over to take a look. He pointed at a picture of himself, a Mac that was some ten years younger.

'That remark of hers did puzzle me a bit, you know when I was introducing myself.'

'So, she knows who you are then?' Leigh said. 'She looks like such a nice woman, why would she be interested in all this?'

'I can think of a good reason, a very good reason indeed,' Mac said with a slow smile.

Chapter Nine

'I see that you've found my little office then,' Kay said cheerily as she placed a tray on the coffee table. 'Here, I've got some nice biscuits for you too.'

Mac and Leigh sat down on the settee.

'Were you having a quick look around while I was out of the room?' Kay asked with a cheeky smile.

'No...well yes, actually,' Mac admitted.

'Just what I'd expect from a good detective.'

'I know your little secret, Mrs. Mathers,' Mac said with a smile as he took a sip of coffee.

'You've found me out have you, DCS Maguire?' Kay said with a broad grin. 'I'd expect no less from you.'

'Found out what?'

Leigh was clearly puzzled.

'We're looking at Letchworth's answer to Agatha Christie, isn't that right Kay?'

'Well I must admit I don't like Agatha Christie that much, all those country house murders. I was going for something much tougher with my writing, more urban if you like, and that's how I knew who you were. I've been doing a lot of research and I've looked at all your cases. Now I get to meet you in person. It's quite exciting really.'

'Tell me, as you're in the business as it were, what's your take on Catherine Gascoigne's murder?' Mac asked.

'Well, I must admit that it's not a storyline I'd have ever come up with. A death in a Jane Austen fan club, not exactly Elmore Leonard, is it?' she said with a wry smile. 'However, I've thought about it quite a bit but I've gotten nowhere, too many suspects perhaps. I think it would be fair to say that Catherine was not a well-liked woman.'

'What about you? Would you have been tempted?'

'Oh no dear,' Kay said with a big smile. 'I found the politics of the Society tiresome but no more than that. When I heard that Anne had formed her own little group I jumped at the chance. For me it's all about the novels, all the little cliques and the manoeuvring that went on in the Janeites almost took the shine off Jane for me.'

'What about the other members of your group?'

'You surely don't suspect one of us, do you?' she said, looking quite serious.

'Not necessarily but I'd still like to know more,' Mac persisted.

'Okay, there's me and there's Anne who runs the group. Then there's Amanda, Molly, Peggy, Diane and Zsuzsanna with a Z. Well two Z's actually.'

'That's an unusual name isn't it?' Mac asked.

'Yes, it is. I think her family were originally from Eastern Europe somewhere.'

'Okay I've already spoken to Anne and Amanda, tell me about the rest.'

Mac didn't want to have to explain what had just happened with Molly. She'd hear about it soon enough. Anyway, he was interested in hearing her opinion of Molly.

'Okay, Molly Etherington never misses a meeting and she really knows her Austen,' Kay replied. 'I suspect that she's a bit of a lonely soul and the meetings are a large part of how she socialises. I don't think she'd say boo to a goose personally. Then there's Peggy Corning. She's like me, getting on a bit. She said that she joined the group to find out more about Austen as her daughter was mad on her. She said once that she lives with her daughter if I remember right. Nice woman, very friendly. And then there's Zsuzsanna Dixon. She's in her fifties and she's very clever. She's deputy head at St. Hilda's School and every bit as good as Catherine when it comes to the scholarly side of Jane's books.

Now Diane Caversham's quite different to the rest of us. She's only thirty or so and already divorced, poor dear. She's always really well dressed and obviously not short of a bob or two. She reads Jane non-stop and I'm sure that if she got an edition that had a full stop in the wrong place then she'd notice it. She left the Society quite acrimoniously apparently, denouncing Catherine as a manipulating bitch in front of all the members. However, she never told us exactly what it was that upset her so much, which is strange isn't it?'

'Tell me more about Diane Caversham,' Mac asked.

He was interested. It seemed that she and Catherine were sworn enemies and he wanted to know why.

'Well, as I said, she's definitely not short of money. She once let it slip that her ex-husband was a banker of some sort.'

'What do you mean by 'let it slip'?' Mac asked.

'Well, that's the only thing I've ever heard her say about her life before she moved here.'

'She lives in Wymondley, doesn't she? How long has she lived there?' Mac asked.

'About eighteen months, I think,' Kay replied. 'She told Anne once that she lived in London before that.'

'What's Diane Caversham like?'

'Well, personally I like her. She's good company usually but there are times when she's a bit prickly, especially when the subject of marriage is raised. I've got the feeling that the break up with her husband might have been a bit on the traumatic side.'

'Any idea why exactly?' Mac asked.

'Not really, she's never talked about her ex-husband, at least as far as I can remember.'

'Well, I'll guess I'll have to ask her myself then, won't I?' Mac said. 'Is there anything else you can tell us that might shed some light on this murder?'

Kay shook her head.

'Sorry but no. Making up plotlines is easy compared to real life, isn't it? This one has me totally stumped.'

'Thanks for your time. I'll leave my number, please ring me if you remember anything that might be relevant.'

'Oh, but before you go can I ask you for a big favour?' Kay asked.

'Of course.'

'Can I buy you a coffee some time? I have some questions about police procedures for my first novel. You could really help.'

'Yes, no problem,' Mac replied. 'You have my number but it would be good if you could leave it for a week or two until...'

'Until you catch the murderer. Yes, I understand completely,' Kay said with a smile. 'Thank you, DCS Maguire.'

Outside Leigh asked, 'Have you ever been in a book before?'

'Yes, I have actually. Just the one but it wasn't a novel, it was about a real case.'

'Well, if I were you,' Leigh said, 'I'd buy Kay's novel if it ever gets published. I'll bet that you'll be in there somewhere. She seems to be quite a fan of yours.'

'Really?' Mac could feel his face start to redden. 'Anyway, let's get on with it.'

Peggy Corning's address was near the golf course and was one of a cluster of small sheltered flats for older people. She wasn't in, a fact that didn't displease Mac at all. The pain in his back was telling him that he desperately needed to get horizontal.

He went straight to the settee when he got home and gratefully lay down. There was a sharp spike of pain that made him yelp but then it started to ebb away as did the feeling of pressure at the bottom of his spine. Before long he felt as if he was floating and it was almost blissful.

He soon drifted off into a dream filled sleep. The dreams were jumbles of things that made no sense except for one, an image so strong that it made him sit bolt upright and, although now wide awake, he could still see it. It seemed to have been seared into his brain.

'Are you alright Mac?' Leigh asked with some concern.

He turned to look at her and shook his head, trying to clear the vision from his eyes.

'How long have I been asleep?' he asked.

'Not long, forty minutes or so. I take it that you don't normally wake up like that. Did you have a bad dream or something?'

'Yes, a dream of sorts, I suppose, and not one that you could describe as good,' he replied as he rubbed the sleep from his eyes. 'While it was just a dream, I can't escape the feeling that my brain is trying to tell me something.'

'What did you dream of?' Leigh asked.

'I saw a woman. It was Philippa Hatch. I mean I haven't seen a photograph of her yet but I knew it was her. She was hanging from the ceiling, her body twisting slowly, but instead of a rope around her neck it was a question mark. It sounds silly, doesn't it?'

'Actually no, it doesn't. You've thought all along that Catherine's murder had something to do with Philippa Hatch's suicide. Perhaps you're just reminding yourself of the fact.'

'I've learned to never ignore messages like that. Anyway, I'd better have a wash and wake myself up.'

'I've done some sandwiches if you're hungry,' Leigh said.

'You're a real star,' Mac said. 'Once I've washed and we've eaten, I'll be ready to go back into the fray. Well here goes.'

He stood up carefully and said a little prayer of thanks, the pain was still there but it was manageable. He gave Leigh the thumbs up.

He checked his phone before leaving the house. There was a message from Andy asking him to drop by the station.

'Have you found something?' Mac asked as he walked into Andy's office.

'Well, technically you did, I suppose. Forensics finally got around to looking at the evidence you got from Catherine Gascoigne's house. Nothing from the stone and only one set of recognisable prints on the key, probably the cleaner's I'd guess. However, have a look at what the envelope contained.'

Andy opened a file on his computer and showed him a photograph. The photograph was of a single sheet of white paper. In big letters right in the centre of the paper it said –

BITCH YOU'RE DEAD

Chapter Ten

It was just three words but Mac was lost in thought for quite a while.

'So, what do you make of that?' Andy eventually asked.

'I'm not sure. Is it a statement or a threat?' Mac replied. 'I take it that you checked the post box when you were there on Sunday?'

'Yes, it was definitely empty then,' Andy replied.

'It was hand posted so I'd guess that it was put in the post box sometime Sunday night. I mean you wouldn't want to be seen posting something like this, would you? I take it that there were no fingerprints or anything else that might help?' Mac asked.

'No prints, standard paper, standard printer so there's very little chance of tracing it that way.'

Mac thought back to the wonderful days of typewriters when you could trace a letter back to a particular machine. Mac was still perplexed though. He was wondering why it was put in the letterbox when Catherine Gascoigne was already dead.

'I take it that nothing like this was found in Mrs. Gascoigne's house?' Mac asked.

Andy shook his head.

'If there were more then she probably burned them. Unfortunately, that's what people tend to do.'

'But she must have told someone about them,' Mac persisted.

'We'll just have to keep asking,' Andy said. 'Anyway, it just confirms what we've been hearing about her. In most murder cases we have to search hard to find people with a motive but in this one there appears to be droves of them.'

As he was getting in the car Leigh asked, 'Where to first? Do you want to go back to Peggy Corning's or shall we try Diane Caversham?'

Mac looked at his watch. It was now two thirty.

'Let's try this Diane Caversham first, she interests me.' Mac looked at the address again. 'You won't need the satnav, just follow the signs to Wymondley. She's in in one of the little row of thatched cottages that are on the right just past the pub. My daughter used to call them the hobbit-houses when she was young. So, she's not all that far from Willian then, where Mrs. Gascoigne lived.'

'Does that have any bearing on the case?'

Mac didn't answer Leigh's question and was quiet as they turned right off the Willian Road.

The row of little black and white cottages with sculpted thatched roofs, beautifully situated in a picture card village, screamed of money to Mac. The names of the cottages were carved on wooden plaques above the front doors which Mac thought was a bit twee. Parr Cottage was one of the end ones. A shiny red Ferrari 458 was parked outside. Mac gave it a long look.

'Why are men always so impressed by sports cars, especially red ones?' Leigh asked.

'It normally takes quite a bit to impress me but then again that's a hell of a lot of car. Come on then, if that's her car then she must be in,' Mac said as he got out.

Amanda rang the bell while Mac gazed admiringly down at the Ferrari. The door was eventually opened by a tall, red haired woman dressed in a silk dressing gown. Mac thought that she was really attractive, except for the fact that she had some redness around the eyes. Mac wondered if she'd been crying for some reason.

Leigh held up her warrant card.

'Come in. I've been expecting you,' she said as she walked back inside the cottage leaving the door open.

Mac followed Leigh inside and looked around. There wasn't much space but what there was of it was tastefully furnished. It had a manly feel to it though. Mac felt as if he'd just stepped into a gentleman's club or something.

'Please sit down,' Diane said with a strained smile, wafting an arm in the general direction of a dark brown leather corner sofa. 'Can I get you anything?'

Mac glanced at the side table next to her chair. It held a full bottle of red wine with the cork out and an empty glass.

'No thank you, Mrs Caversham...' Mac said.

'Oh, please call me Diane and by the way it's Miss Caversham, it's my maiden name. I was married but I didn't want to keep anything of that bastard I was married to and that included his name,' she said with some vitriol.

'Okay, Diane,' Mac said. 'We're investigating the murder of Catherine Gascoigne. I take it that you've heard that her death was murder?'

Diane nodded.

'News travels fast around here.'

'Is there anything you can tell us that might help?' Mac asked.

'No, I'm sorry but I haven't seen Catherine for ages,' Diane replied. 'Although, if I'm being honest, I wasn't sorry about that at all. On the whole I've been very grateful that she's kept herself out of my way.'

Mac looked closely at Diane as she talked. Her long hair was uncombed and she looked like she'd been living in her dressing gown for a few days.

'Yes, I've heard that you and Catherine didn't get on. Why was that though?'

'Well, she was just a cow, wasn't she? A bully too, I hate bullies.'

'Who did Catherine bully?' Mac asked.

'Well me for one, or at least she tried. Then there was Molly and poor Pippa Hatch and I know Anne fell out with her about something. Believe me, there's a long, long list. Her latest victim was Ginny Hocking, really shocking that was.'

'Who's Ginny Hocking?' Mac asked.

'I'm not sure how long she'd been a member of the Society but she was definitely there before I joined,' Diane replied. 'Anyway, Ginny had a bit of a falling out with Catherine a couple of months ago, about ball dates or something. I heard it all got a bit acrimonious and then Ginny led a bit of a revolt and nearly won the vote. That really put Catherine's nose out of joint. The only problem was that Ginny made the mistake of going on holiday because when she got back there was a letter waiting for her telling her she's been kicked out of the Society. Well, she went ballistic and even wrote a letter to the local paper about it comparing Catherine to Stalin. It's a real pity that they didn't print it.'

'How did you hear about this?'

'I had Ginny over for a bottle of wine a week or two ago and she told me about it herself,' Diane replied. 'I should have said a bottle or two as we both got quite squiffy.'

'What else did she say?' Mac asked.

Diane hesitated. Mac could see that she was debating with herself about something.

'Oh, I suppose that she'll tell you herself anyway. We were daydreaming about killing Catherine and how we'd do it. She said she favoured the toaster in the bath as the best option or running her over ...'

She stopped talking. A thought had obviously occurred to her. She didn't seem to be in any hurry to share it though.

'Or what?' Mac eventually prompted.

'Or poisoning her,' she eventually replied.

'Do you know where this Ginny Hocking lives and her phone number, if you have it?'

'Yes, of course. I'll get my address book.'

While Diane was out of the room Leigh whispered, 'This Ginny might make a good suspect then.'

'Perhaps, but my first question is what's Diane telling us all this for? Is she trying to divert attention from herself? I've got a strong feeling that she's hiding something.'

At that moment Diane returned and gave Mac a sheet of paper torn from a notebook. She gave it to him with some reluctance. Mac wondered if she was having second thoughts about telling him about Ginny Hocking.

'Where were you the night that Catherine was murdered?' Mac asked.

'Here by myself, as usual.'

'That's unfortunate,' Mac said.

'Yes, it is, isn't it? There's never a man around when you need one, not even for an alibi.'

Mac thought he saw the glimmer of a tear drop in the corner of her eye.

'Tell me is that your car outside, the Ferrari?'

'Yes.'

'Is that the only car you have access to?'

Diane looked mystified.

'Yes, why would I need another one?'

'Diane, have you ever heard of thallium?'

Mac could sense a more than momentary hesitation.

'Thallium? No, I don't recall ever hearing the word,' she replied.

Leigh noticed Mac looking intently at Diane with a look of puzzlement on his face.

'Let's return to you and Catherine,' Mac said. 'Why didn't you two get on?'

'As I said she was bully. I had enough of those when I was at school.'

'Yes, you've already said that but I think there's a bit more to it than that, isn't there Diane?'

'What other reason could there be?'

'Is it true that you denounced Catherine at one of the Society's meetings?' Mac asked.

'Well, it's true that we did have a bit of a slanging match,' Diane replied. 'I resigned afterwards, I got my letter in quick before they could hold a meeting and kick me out.'

'Why did you have a slanging match though? It must have been about something important to have caused such an outburst.'

'No, it was just a build-up of things,' she replied without much conviction. 'I suppose we just rubbed each other up the wrong way.'

'But there was something though, wasn't there? Something very specific,' Mac said as he gave her a sceptical look.

She didn't reply but Mac could see from her reaction that he was on the right track.

'Diane, please remember that this is a murder enquiry,' he warned.

She got up and started pacing up and down. Her decision made she sat down and said, 'Yes there was something, something very specific. Nico.'

'Is that Nico Panagos you're referring to, the head waiter at the Earl Lewin?'

Diane nodded. She had a rueful expression on her face.

'I met Nico about a year ago and we had a little...er...I don't know what you'd call it.'

'An affair?' Mac suggested.

'A sort of an affair, I suppose.'

Diane looked up to the ceiling. From her face Mac could see that she wasn't especially proud of what she was about to tell them.

'I got lonely being here all by myself so I used to go to the Earl Lewin a lot and that's how I got to know Nico. He's a very good-looking man and so I made him a proposition.'

The light bulb went on in Mac's head.

'You paid him for sex,' he stated.

Diane looked a little agitated.

'Well, I wouldn't have put it quite that bluntly but yes, I suppose.'

'So, what happened?' Mac asked.

'Well, after one of the Society's meetings we all got a bit drunk and they started talking about men and sex and that kind of thing. Catherine virtually accused me of either being asexual or a lesbian and so I told her about the beautiful young man who serviced me. I didn't name names but I did mention the Earl Lewin so I guess it wasn't hard for her to figure out that it was Nico. Anyway, a couple of weeks later she made him an offer he seemingly couldn't refuse. A month or so after that he told me that he didn't have the energy for two women as well as his wife so that was the end of him and me. He was very sweet about it.'

'I'd guess that you didn't take that well,' Mac said.

She gave him a shame-faced look.

'You're right there, I definitely didn't. At the next meeting Catherine and I had a big fight. They had to hold me back, I so wanted to punch her lights out.'

'Is there anything else you can tell me?'

'About Catherine, no,' Diane said. 'We never met again after that meeting.'

After a few more questions Mac and Leigh took their leave. As they showed themselves out, he saw Diane put the cork back in the bottle of wine. She looked desperately sad as she did this.

Once in the car Mac asked, 'So what do you think?'

'Well, speaking as a woman, I'd say that's more than enough motive for murder,' Leigh replied.

100

'Yes, I've known people kill for a hell of a lot less. Come on, let's see if this Peggy Corning's come home yet.'

Leigh drove them back towards Willian. She turned left and then right up Letchworth Lane past the golf club and parked outside the retirement flats. Mac rang Peggy Corning's bell but again got no answer.

A head popped out of the window next door and a grey-haired woman said, 'There's no-one home. He's gone to his daughter's house for the week.'

'He?' Mac asked. 'I thought that a woman lived here.'

'No, Mr. Mann's been living there for over six months, ever since Peggy left.'

'Is that Peggy Corning you're talking about? She's the person I'm looking for.'

Mac showed the woman his card. She disappeared and a few seconds later the front door opened.

'What would the police want with Peggy?' she said. 'She's a really nice lady.'

'It's just routine,' Mac replied. 'You say that she moved out six months ago, do you know where to?'

'I'm sorry no,' she said with a shake of her head. 'I think she might have left a forwarding address with the warden though.'

'Why did she move, do you know?'

'Well, she said that she was moving back in with her daughter. She'd let her have the house when she got married and Peggy moved in here. The marriage didn't take though and her daughter wanted her to move back. I suppose she was a bit lonely being there all by herself.'

'How can I contact this warden?' Mac asked.

'She lives there', the woman said pointing to the flat opposite, 'but she won't be back until tomorrow sometime.'

Mac's phone went off.

'Thanks,' he said to the woman.

He then turned and answered the phone.

All Leigh heard was 'Really! Yes, we'll be there in ten minutes.'

He ended the call and turned to her.

'Come on, Olivia Parker's been found dead in her house and they're pretty sure that she's been poisoned!'

Another poisoning

He had to admit that he had finally found his calling. He'd expanded his operations to neighbouring towns and even as far as London. His friend Mr. T hadn't been rumbled once as he went quietly and efficiently about his work.

He read the papers avidly and never missed the news as he was always on the lookout for his next project. His latest though proved to be much closer to home.

He'd come back one evening to find his wife really upset. She'd had a visit from a friend of hers who lived a few streets away. This friend had shown up at their house before with black eyes and bruised arms always, she said, after walking into several doors. His wife had advised her friend numerous times to leave her husband but she said she couldn't, she was too scared of him.

During this last visit she'd tearfully admitted that her husband had now started on their son. He'd beaten the child black and blue with his belt because he'd wet the bed. Her son was five years old.

His wife had cried as she told him this and he comforted her. Five years old. That alone decided him. He told his wife it would be alright and not to worry, it would all work out for the best. He didn't tell her about his friend though, the one who could cure all earthly ills.

When he researched further, everything he discovered only served to confirm his original feelings. The man was a drunk and a lout, a slug with no redeeming features at all. No-one had a good word to say about him but they would never say this to his face. He was a big man, a mean man with a very uncertain temper.

He worked in a garage and, when not there, he spent all his time in the pub. He'd found what the slug's favourite drink was and made his plans. He reminded himself to keep it simple as always.

It was no co-incidence that late one evening he had stationed himself on the route that the slug took when he finally decided to go home from the pub. He sat on a wall and beside him there stood an unopened bottle of beer. The slug swayed around the corner and came to a stop when he saw the bottle. He could see the slug's desire for the contents of the bottle in his eyes.

The slug made an attempt to smile but it came out as a sneer. He attempted some small talk but it soon led to his real purpose.

'Are you going to drink that?' he asked pointing to the bottle.

He shrugged and said he wasn't sure. He said he'd never tried that beer before.

The slug told him that he wouldn't like it and that he'd be more than happy to take it off his hands. He tried to protest when the slug snatched the bottle.

The slug glared menacingly at him and said, 'I said you wouldn't like it. Don't you believe me, pal?'

The emphasis on the 'pal' assured him that he was anything but that. He meekly assented to the slug taking the bottle away. A few yards down the road the slug knocked the cap off on a wall and took a big swig. He could hear the slug laughing as he walked away.

'You've got no insides pal, no guts,' the slug shouted back at him.

He smiled. His guts were fine and would be staying right where they were. As for the slug's, well...he figured that they'd be keeping the worms happy for some considerable time to come.

Chapter Eleven

Besides the old Land Rover there were two police cars, a forensics van and an ambulance in the driveway. There was still plenty of room left for Leigh to park their car in. Just as Mac was getting out another car pulled up and Andy Reid and Toni Woodgate got out.

'We were the other side of Stotfold when we heard the news,' Andy explained. 'It looks like forensics have beaten us to it. Come on let's see what they've found.'

They followed Andy up a wide staircase. Mac held on tight to the bannister and went up slowly, looking down at his feet. Leigh slowed down when she noticed he was lagging behind.

'I think they went in there,' Leigh said, pointing to a door when they finally reached the landing.

Two men in plastic coveralls hovered around a bed while a third stood talking to Andy and Toni.

Andy turned around.

'Mac, this is Bob Yeardley.'

'Yes, we met at Molly Etherington's,' Mac replied.

'We'd only just finished up there when we got the call for this one. It saved us some petrol, I suppose,' Bob said.

'Was it a poisoning?' Mac asked.

'That's what we think,' Bob replied. 'However, I wouldn't get too excited as I doubt it was thallium that was used, although we'll do the full tox screen just in case.'

At this point one of the forensics men moved and Mac could see Olivia's body. She was fully clothed and lying on her left side. The pillow was stained with vomit. Mac had seen this sight many times before.

'What do you think she took?' Mac asked.

In his younger days, barbiturates had been the drug of choice but they were hard to get these days.

'Anti-depressants mostly. There was an empty bottle next to the bed as well as two empty packets of paracetamol and one of co-proxamol plus a nearly empty bottle of vodka.'

'So, she was serious about killing herself then,' Mac commented.

'Is there any chance of this not being suicide?' Andy asked.

'Well she did have some bruising to the face. It looks like someone hit her a few times,' Bob replied. 'It's still probably suicide though, there was a note.'

Bob led them into the bathroom. On a large mirror over the hand basin the words 'I hope you're happy now!!!' were scrawled in black. The marker pen was still in the basin.

'Her writing?' Andy asked.

'We found a diary in one of the drawers and yes, the writing looks the same. We'll need to get that properly verified of course.'

'The diary, did it explain why she might want to have killed herself?' Mac asked.

'Possibly, do you know anything about a computer? She wrote something about if her husband hadn't been such a miser and bought her a new computer when she'd asked, all this might have been avoided. As it was written yesterday, I'm assuming that she's referring to her suicide.'

'I need to make a call,' Andy said.

He turned and walked out onto the landing.

Mac remembered the last time he'd seen Olivia Parker and the worried expression she'd had on her face after he'd told her how indestructible hard drives could be. It was Mac's guess that Andy was talking to the computer specialist right now to see what he'd found on the computer.

'Who found her?' Mac asked.

'The cleaner,' Bob replied. 'I think she's waiting downstairs in the kitchen if you want to talk to her.'

Andy returned and Mac could tell from the surprised expression on his face that he'd been told something that he hadn't been expecting.

'You'll never guess!' Andy said excitedly. 'Remember those encrypted files that computer forensics found on the hard drive? Well, they broke the encryption and they turned out to be very interesting, interesting enough that they sent them straight on to the Financial Intelligence Unit. Too sensitive for us ordinary plods to get a look at, although they did give me an idea of what it was all about.'

'And?' Mac couldn't help saying.

He was really intrigued as to what could have been on the computer.

'Bribes,' Andy stated.

'Bribes?' Mac replied, none the wiser. 'I thought that the FIU were more interested in terrorism and money laundering.'

'Mr. Parker has a business that sells weapons for military jets, apparently he specialises in air launched missiles and torpedoes,' Andy explained. 'The files that were encrypted related to large sums of money paid to Middle Eastern middle-men, bribes for military contracts. Some of these middle-men are also well-known supporters of terrorism.'

'So, the bribes may well have gone straight into the terrorist's coffers. What have the FIU done?'

'They've alerted all the airports and ports to be on the look-out for George Parker,' Andy replied. 'They know that he entered the country yesterday morning and, as far as they can tell, he hasn't left yet. I still can't understand how Mr. Parker would ever allow his wife to use a computer that had such damning evidence on it. And why did she say in her diary that it was all her husband's fault for not buying her a new computer?'

107

'I have an idea about that,' Mac said, 'but I think we'd be better off speaking to someone who might know for sure. Shall we have a word with the cleaner first though?'

They found her in the kitchen, a small Indian woman with an apron on. She sat at a table, wide-eyed and cradling a mug of tea in her hands.

'I believe that you found Mrs. Parker?' Andy asked.

She nodded glumly.

'Yes, I knew she was in because of the car. When I first saw her, I thought that she might have had a headache and that's why she was in bed during the day. She used to get migraines sometimes. Then I saw the vomit and...'

She started shaking and took a sip of the tea to calm herself down.

'Have you any idea why she might have wanted to kill herself?' Andy asked.

'She had a big row with her husband yesterday. They were upstairs but I could hear it down here.'

'What was it about?' Andy asked.

'I'm not sure, I could hear their voices but not the words. He was really angry while she was sort of pleading with him. Then he left slamming the door behind him.'

'Do you know if Mr. Parker hit his wife?' Andy asked.

She nodded glumly again.

'After I heard them fighting, she came down and one side of her face was all red and puffing up.'

As she couldn't add anything else Andy thanked her and took her name and address.

Outside Andy asked, 'So, who is this person who might know?'

'The last Musketeer,' Mac said.

Penny Bathurst answered the door herself this time and from the looks on Andy and Mac's faces she could tell that something serious had happened.

'Oh God, it's not Olivia, is it?' she asked.

Andy nodded.

Penny burst into tears and turned away from the door. Mac and Andy followed her inside.

In between the sobs they could hear her saying in a low voice, 'I should have done something.'

Mac found a bell on the table and rang it. A few seconds later the maid appeared. Mac asked her to bring a cup of tea for her employer and some tissues.

Penny cradled the cup while she drank, its warmth against the palms of her hands was soothing in itself. Mac had learned to never underestimate the comfort that a simple cup of tea could bring. When she'd finished, she placed the cup carefully on the table and looked at the two men.

'She's killed herself, hasn't she?'

Both Mac and Andy nodded.

'I knew something bad would happen, I just knew it. I offered to stay the night to keep her company but she wouldn't hear of it. She told me that she was feeling better, that she was alright. I shouldn't have believed her, should I?' Penny said as she dabbed a tissue at her eyes and then blew her nose.

'Tell us exactly what happened,' Andy asked gently.

'I got a phone call from Olivia yesterday afternoon begging me to come around immediately. Her husband had come home on one of his rare visits. It had been on her mind so much that she told him about the laptop almost as soon as he'd come in the door. He went absolutely ballistic, hit her several times and then picked up his bags and left. He told her that she'd never see him again. Unfortunately for Olivia she was still very much in love with him, even though he was such a total bastard.'

'Why do you call him that?' Mac asked.

He wanted to know more about this George Parker.

'When he was younger, he was a very good-looking man, he still is I suppose,' Penny replied. 'Anyway, he swept Olivia off her feet. He was attentive and charming, not just to her, but to all her family as well. Everyone loved George. It was a lovely wedding too and we were all so jealous of Olivia. That jealousy didn't last long though. It became crystal clear within a couple of months that it was her money that he'd been interested in, not her. He used it to start his business up and then she started seeing less and less of him. He gave her an allowance to live on, can you believe that? Two hundred pounds a week. She'd been worth millions when she married him and yet there she was, always asking Catherine and myself for loans so she could pay the cleaner or get petrol. She never blamed him though. She still loved him and that I suppose was the real problem.'

'Can we go back a bit,' Andy asked. 'The computer, how did Olivia come by it?'

'Well, last year George came back on a flying visit and, while he was here, he bought himself a flashy new laptop. Olivia was getting by with one that was really on its way out so she asked him if she could have his old one. He told her that she'd just have to make the old one last a bit longer as his computer was being picked up by someone the next day. He'd left Olivia strict instructions that when the man arrived, she was to hand him the computer which he'd packed in a box...'

'Let me guess,' Mac interrupted, 'she switched computers and sent her old one off instead. I take it that the computer was being sent off to have its memory wiped before being destroyed?'

'Yes, she thought she'd get one over on him and anyway she said she could delete everything herself and wondered why George would need to pay someone to do it.'

'She wasn't exactly an IT expert, was she?' Andy commented.

'Unfortunately for her, no,' Penny replied. 'She told me the whole story after you visited her Mr. Maguire.

She thought that you might have been joking when you said that you'd still be able to get all the information off the hard drive, even after what she'd done to it. We asked an expert and he told her that you were right. I've never seen her look so worried.'

'What else did she say yesterday?' Mac prompted.

'Not much, apart from telling me that I was a real friend and that she now realised that mine and Catherine's friendship had been the most important thing in her life. She'd never said anything like that before and I must admit that it worried me. However, she seemed to calm down, in fact she was almost icily calm when I left her. I guess that's because she'd already made her mind up, hadn't she? I went around there first thing this morning but no-one answered the door. Now I know why, she was already dead.'

Penny burst into tears again.

'Is there anyone we can call?' Andy asked.

Penny shook her head and gave them a desolate look.

'I've been married twice and found out too late that they were both like George. The only people I've ever been really close to, the only people who really cared about me, well they're both dead now.'

Andy and Mac were both quiet as they got back into the car. Mac had a thought.

'Can we stop by the library? I'll only be a moment.'

Mac disappeared for a minute and came back accompanied by a flustered and concerned looking Anne Holding.

'Would it be okay if we drop Anne here at Penny Bathurst's?'

Andy was more than happy to oblige. They then returned to Olivia Parker's house and met up with Toni and Leigh. As it was now well past five o'clock, they agreed that it might be best to go back to the station and go over what they'd found to date.

Andy had spent the day visiting members of the Society who'd had run-ins in the past with Catherine Gascoigne. However, no-one was crowing about her death and, like Anne, they all seemed to be more shocked than anything else.

Mac told Andy and Toni of their meetings with Kay Mathers and Diane Caversham. Andy seemed to be particularly interested in Diane.

'It looks as if she's got a motive and, with her living so close to Catherine Gascoigne, probably the opportunity too. But what about the means?'

'Yes, that's the sticking point, isn't it? Where could she, or anyone, have gotten thallium from?' Mac asked.

'It might be worth doing some checking on her though,' Andy said.

'I agree. She also mentioned a Ginny Hocking, another ex-member with a grudge apparently. After a few drinks a couple of weeks ago she said that she wanted to murder Catherine Gascoigne and discussed how she'd do it. One of them was poison, at least that's what Diane says.'

'It's not something you're likely to say if you're serious about murdering someone though, is it? I'll check her out tomorrow anyway. I've seen her name on my list.'

'Here's her phone number.'

Mac gave Andy the sheet of paper Diane had given him.

Andy looked at Mac for a few seconds and then said, 'Come on, Mac tell me, I've seen that expression before. Have you got any suspicions about Diane Caversham?'

'I'm just wondering why Diane told me about Ginny Hocking,' Mac replied. 'I can't get rid of the feeling that she's trying to deflect attention away from herself for some reason, that's all.'

'Okay, if you two concentrate on Diane Caversham tomorrow then we'll go and see this Ginny Hocking,'

Andy said. 'They're the nearest thing to suspects that we have at the moment. Let's knock off for the day, I'll see you all back here at nine tomorrow.'

Andy walked with Mac to the door.

'Get some rest Mac,' he said. 'You look really tired.'

Mac had been hoping that it wasn't so noticeable.

'Don't worry, I've already texted Tim and told him the pub's off for tonight. It's straight to bed for me once I've had a bite to eat.'

Toni caught up with them.

'Mac, this came for you.'

She handed Mac a large thick brown envelope. Mac guessed that it was Philippa Hatch's file. He'd read it later.

Leigh dropped him home. He found that he didn't have the appetite or the strength to make anything to eat. The pain was definitely getting the upper hand. He changed his patch and took two little blue pills that he knew would knock him out for a minimum of twelve hours.

Sleep mercifully came quite quickly.

Chapter Twelve

Wednesday

He waded through a sea of surreal dreams and images as he made his way back towards full consciousness. He turned on the light and glanced at the clock. It was nearly seven o'clock. Although he was still somewhat groggy, he was aware of having had a good night's sleep and was more than grateful for it. He sat up and then stood up expecting the worst. He smiled when he only felt the normal pain levels.

His stomach was rumbling as he shaved and he realised that he was absolutely ravenous. He remembered that he hadn't eaten the evening before and the thought of a Full English breakfast was irresistible. The Magnets opened at eight and he decided he was going to order the biggest breakfast they had.

As he had some time, he went to the cemetery first and told Nora all about the case. Telling her helped him put everything in some sort of order in his head. His stomach rumbled loudly and he heard her say 'Oh go and get yourself something to eat, you eejit.' When she called him an 'eejit' it was always said softly and with a smile. He smiled, said good-bye and headed off to the Magnets.

After a very satisfying Full English, he caught Andy and Toni in the corridor of the police station as they were on their way out.

'You're looking much better today,' Andy said.

'I'm feeling much better too,' Mac replied. 'It's wonderful what a good night's sleep and a good breakfast can do for you.'

'It's just as well, two of the team are out with flu today and we've had another spate of burglaries last night. Unfortunately, one of them was at the house of a county councillor so there'll be hell to pay if we don't start making some real progress. I've got my best people on it but I could do with wrapping this murder case up as soon as possible. So, for lots of reasons I'm really glad you're okay.'

'Thanks. I take it you're on your way to see Ginny Hocking?' Mac asked.

'Yes, I just rang her and she's happy to see us now. Are you going to do some digging on Diane Caversham?'

'That's the plan. Do you want to compare notes when you get back?' Mac suggested.

'Absolutely, we'll see you later.'

Mac had no problem finding a free desk and computer. Andy's team really were really thin on the ground that morning. By the time Leigh arrived Mac had already found the answer to something that had been bugging him since his interview with Diane.

'Do you remember me asking Diane if she'd ever heard about thallium?'

'Yes, and I remember that you looked at her in quite a strange way when she said that she'd never heard of it,' Leigh said.

'That's because I knew she was lying. I didn't know just how much of a lie it was until just now though.'

'What have you found?' she asked.

Mac pointed to the computer screen.

'Google is a truly wonderful thing if you're a policeman. Years ago, it would have taken a hell of a lot of shoe leather to find this out.'

Leigh peered at the screen.

'This is a Wikipedia article about Simon Alders Caversham. Who's he?' she asked.

'He founded the Caversham Chemical Company.'

'I've never heard of them,' Leigh said.

'You might know them better as 3C.'

'God, they're massive, aren't they? I see their lorries all over the place. I take it that this Simon Caversham is something to Diane then?'

'He was her father, he died six years ago,' Mac said. 'I'll just scroll down a bit to another photo. There's someone in it who you might recognise.'

Leigh peered at the photo.

'God, yes that's definitely Diane standing next to him. She's really young there but what's she doing in a white coat and why is she holding a test tube?'

'It wasn't just for show. Here's something else I found.'

Mac opened another page.

'It's one of the Cambridge alumni associations,' Leigh said with some surprise. She read it out loud, 'Diane Caversham, Secretary, Trinity Gas Group. What does that mean?' she asked.

'The Trinity Gas Group is for people who got degrees in Chemistry at Trinity College. Apparently, Diane left with a first-class degree.'

'And she said that she'd never heard of thallium!' Leigh exclaimed. 'I have to admit that I'm surprised though. Looking at her, I'd have guessed that she'd have done something fluffy at university like History of Art or something. A first at Chemistry though, she wasn't just lying, she was lying through her teeth.'

'The question now is why?' Mac said. 'Before we ask her that question let's do a little more digging. I've just started looking at the information that Companies House has on 3C. Let's see what they've got.'

They both peered at the screen together.

'Look,' Leigh said excitedly. 'Here.'

She pointed at the screen.

'It says here that Diane Caversham is a Director of 3C. I wonder if we can find out if she owns any shares?'

'I think that might be a bit difficult to find on the internet but I know a man who can,' Mac said.

While he made his call, Leigh continued wading through Google. She found that thallium is mostly used in photo-electric cells and the specialist glass industry.

She wasn't at all surprised to learn that one of the biggest manufacturers of thallium sulphide and thallium oxide in the UK was a company called 3C.

Mac came back with a look of surprise on his face.

'I know this financial journalist and he reeled the figures off the top of his head. Apparently, Diane owns about fifteen per cent of the company, so at the current share price she's worth well over a hundred and fifty million.'

Leigh raised her eyebrows.

'That's a serious amount of money.'

'There's more,' Mac said. 'He also told me that there's a takeover by an even bigger US company in the wind and Diane's shares are the key as to whether it succeeds or not. If she sells, she might get two or even three times the current share price.'

Mac heard a low rumbling sound coming from outside and noticed that some members of the team were gravitating towards the windows overlooking the car park. He joined them and watched Diane as she expertly parked the Ferrari 458. As she walked away a small crowd gathered around the car, all gazing admiringly down at its glossy red paintwork.

He turned to Leigh, 'You can see now why I asked Diane if she had access to any other cars. If she'd have driven that in the middle of the night to murder Catherine then she'd have woken most of Willian up. Come on let's see what she wants.'

Mac intercepted Diane in the lobby.

'Do you want to speak to me formally?' he asked.

After a pause she nodded her head.

Mac spoke to the police constable manning the reception desk who pointed him towards an empty interview room.

He ushered Diane into the room and a few seconds later they were joined by Leigh. Mac turned on the recorder and stated the time and date.

'Civilian consultant Mac Maguire and DC Marston are interviewing…' Mac paused and looked at Diane. 'Please state your full name and address.'

Diane did so.

'Okay, before we start how would you like me to address you?' Mac asked.

'Diane will be fine.'

'I would like to state here that Diane Caversham has come to the police station by her own volition and has stated that she wished to attend a formal interview.'

Mac thought he might as well cut to the chase.

'Okay Diane, do you recall that in an informal interview yesterday I asked if you'd ever heard of thallium?'

Diane nodded.

'Sorry, can you say yes or no, we're only recording the sound.'

'Sorry, yes, yes I remember you asking me,' Diane said a little too loudly.

'And how did you answer?'

She paused before answering. Mac gave her time as he felt she was making some sort of a final decision. Her shoulders relaxed and Mac knew she'd made a choice.

'I said that I'd never heard of it.'

'That was a lie wasn't it?' Mac stated.

'Yes, it was a lie. I could tell you quite a lot about thallium, its position in the periodic table, eighty one and that it's a post-transition metal. It's incredibly toxic and only used nowadays in glass manufacturing and electronics. The biggest manufacturer of thallium derivatives is the company my father founded and in which I'm a director. And yes, I could lay my hands on enough thallium to kill half of England if I wanted. Is that enough for now?'

'More than enough,' Mac said. 'Why did you lie, Diane?'

Another pause for thought, then she got her phone out of her handbag and turned it on.

'Because I know that I'm probably suspect number one and that I'll be even more so after you see this. It came yesterday morning.'

She passed the phone to Mac. A video was playing. It was night and the video was clearly being taken by someone sitting in a car. Diane could be seen opening the door of 'The Earl Lewin' pub and then walking down the road towards Catherine's house. Whoever was taking the video also got out of their car and followed her on the other side of the road. She walked down a drive and the camera followed her. She stopped in front of a house and a sign with 'The Old Alms House Anno Domini 1641' was clearly visible. Diane then walked up to the front door and at that point the video stopped.

'Look at the time stamp,' Diane said.

Mac did. It was nine thirty in the evening and it was the night before Catherine had been found dead.

'Someone's blackmailing you,' Mac stated.

Diane nodded, she looked close to tears.

'It's this stupid bloody takeover,' she said. 'They're trying everything to get me to sell my shares but I know what they'll do if I sell. They'll asset strip the company and close most of it down. Yes, I could make a nice chunk of money but my father spent his whole life building that company up and I'll be damned...anyway, that's why I lied. I was so scared, what is it I always hear on the TV in the police shows...motive, means and opportunity? Well I have all those in spades, don't I?'

'I take it that they've had people following you,' Mac said.

Diane nodded.

'Why didn't you tell me this yesterday?' Mac asked.

'I was in a bit of a panic I suppose and, if I'm honest, that's why I mentioned my conversation with Ginny. That was really beneath me. Ginny did say those words but she was drunk and she didn't mean it. I suppose that I was being bloody naïve too, hoping somehow that it would all just go away. Then after we spoke and I'd calmed down a bit, I thought of how easy it would be to find out about 3C, the chemistry degree and all the other things. I knew that it wasn't going to go away after all.'

'Did you poison Catherine Gascoigne?' Mac asked.

'No, no I didn't,' Diane replied looking Mac right in the eye. 'Although I must admit that the thought had crossed my mind more than once. I know it looks bad for me but I need you to believe that.'

Mac did. He'd already figured that, with all her knowledge, she'd at least have gotten the dosage right and wouldn't need several goes at it. He said nothing about that though.

'What were you doing at Catherine's house the night before she died?'

Diane heaved a huge sigh.

'I guess that no-one will believe me but I wanted to make peace. I wanted to bury the hatchet and, for once, not in her head. I needed to end the war, for the sake of 3C.'

'What did Catherine have to do with 3C?'

'She owned just under one per cent of the company, the shares were originally bought by her husband some time ago. They're good solid performers, a lot of the pension funds and the like have bought into the company for which I'm eternally grateful. If they hadn't, we'd have lost the company by now.'

'Why is that?' Mac asked.

'Because they're in it for the long term, they're not so interested in a quick kill now but in providing income for pensioners thirty years from now. If AMMI get their hands on it the company won't last long.'

'Who or what is AMMI?' Mac asked.

'Sorry, they're an American company, the Alaskan Mining and Manufacturing Industries Corporation,' Diane explained. 'They started out in mining but they've got interests in just about everything now and they're incredibly cash-rich at the moment. Unfortunately, they've chosen 3C to throw some of their money at. Anyway, things are so evenly balanced that Catherine's holdings, small as they were, could well make the difference.'

'Of course, you realise that if we find that Catherine was thinking of selling her shares to AMMI then this gives you yet another motive for killing her?' Mac said.

'It's not looking good for me, is it?' she said with a grimace.

'The video ends with you at Catherine's door. What happened after that?'

Diane shrugged.

'Nothing, she never answered the door and so I went back home.'

'Good,' Mac said. 'I noticed when I was there that the pub has CCTV cameras on the front entrance and the car park and they might help to confirm your story. Who do you think is behind this blackmail attempt?'

'It's going to be one of the underlings at AMMI but which one is anyone's guess.'

Mac gave this some thought.

'Who sent it? I mean was there an email address or something?'

'It was sent from a social site by someone called '3C or not 3C'. Some joke,' she said almost getting tearful again.

'Is there anything else you can tell me that might be relevant to Catherine Gascoigne's murder?'

Diane shook her head.

'No, I'm sorry and I'm being absolutely truthful this time.'

Mac stood up and held out his hand.

'Diane, thanks for coming to see us today. You've been most helpful.'

She looked quite puzzled as she shook his hand.

'Is that it? I half thought I'd be, oh what do they call it on the TV? Yes 'banged up'. Aren't you even going to tell me not to leave the country?'

'You're not thinking of leaving the country, are you?'

'Well no but...'

'Well that's fine then,' Mac said with a smile. 'We'll be in touch if we need anything else.'

He watched Diane as she walked away from him down the hall. For all her money, intelligence and good looks she was a bit of a sad case.

'Do you think she did it?' Leigh asked.

Mac shook his head.

'No, I don't think it's her but it's given me an idea of who it might be though. Can we wait until Andy and Toni get back? I just need to think it through a bit. Let's see if we can find out a bit more about this AMMI though.'

It didn't take them long. It was clear that the company was both incredibly rich and powerful. Then they hit gold dust when they stumbled upon an article from the New York Times. The article described the divorce proceedings between one of AMMI's major shareholders, Alix Stefanovic, and his wife Diane. It was Leigh who spotted the photo.

'Look it's her!' she said excitedly.

The photo showed a woman walking up the steps to an old building, a court house Mac guessed. Although she was wearing sunglasses it was definitely Diane.

From the article they learned that the couple had only been married for two years when Diane had started divorce proceedings. The hearings had all taken place in the US and it seemed to have been quite acrimonious. Mac could understand why. The reason Diane had wanted out of her marriage was that she'd caught her husband in bed with her best friend. Apparently, he'd been cheating on her since before they were married and she had proof.

'It just gets more interesting doesn't it?' Mac said. 'Perhaps Philippa Hatch had nothing to do with it after all.'

Andy and Toni walked into the room. Their jackets were wet and they dripped as they hung them on the coat stand.

'Did you get anything from Ginny Hocking?' Mac asked.

Andy shook his head.

'She was quite honest about her dislike of Catherine Gascoigne and she also admitted that she may have discussed murdering her with Diane Caversham. She said she was quite drunk at the time and they were just having a bit of fun. Fortunately for her, she has a cast iron alibi for around the time Catherine died. She was on holiday in Morocco and she's got the videos to prove it. I'm hoping that you did a bit better.'

'I think we did,' Mac replied. 'We found out quite a bit about Diane Caversham from the internet and even more from Diane herself.'

'She was here?' Andy said looking surprised.

'Yes, she came in voluntarily. She admitted lying to me yesterday but I can understand it in a way. She got a first in Chemistry and she's also a director of 3C, the chemical company. Through them she has access to enough thallium, in her own words, 'to poison half of England'.'

'Yet I get the strange feeling that you don't fancy her for the murder,' Andy said.

'No, I don't. The main reasons are that she would have known the lethal dosage and would have gotten it right first time and again, like Molly Etherington, why wait such a long time to get revenge?'

'But you do fancy someone, don't you?' Andy ventured.

'Perhaps I do,' Mac said. 'The use of thallium really had me flummoxed if I'm honest. Why use a poison that's so hard to get? Then I remembered a case from only a few years ago in America where a man died and thallium was finally identified as the cause. His wife was a chemist and she was convicted of his murder. It could only have been her as only she had access to the poison. Anyway, it made quite a stir in the US and this set me thinking. What if Catherine wasn't killed for anything she'd done or said, what if she was killed just to put Diane in the frame?'

Andy leant forward, 'Go on.'

'3C was founded by Diane's father and, as I said, she's a director. We found out that its future is threatened as an American company called Alaskan Mining and Manufacturing is trying to engineer a hostile takeover. Now, it would be all too easy for anyone to put together the facts that Diane hated Catherine and that she also had access to thallium. So, if you wanted Diane out of the way, poison Catherine and Diane has to be the obvious suspect.'

'What makes you think this mining company might be involved?' Tony asked.

'I think Leigh's got a bigger phone. Has it come though yet?' Mac asked.

'Yes, here it is.'

Leigh held up her phone and played the short video.

'This was sent to Diane on the morning of the day I interviewed her,' Mac said. 'I can well believe that it might have rattled her which is also probably why she lied.'

Andy watched the short video twice.

'So, she's got a motive, access to the poison used and this video proves that she was on Catherine Gascoigne's door step the night before was found dead. It's really neat, isn't it?'

'A bit too neat for my liking,' Mac replied. 'It looks as if someone from this American company is trying to blackmail Diane into selling 3C but would they stoop to murder? I'm not sure but I think that it might be well worth looking into.'

Andy didn't look convinced.

'Yes, but it's a bit unlikely, isn't it?'

'I'd agree, corporations and takeovers can be seen to be a bit impersonal and murders are usually very personal acts,' Mac said. 'However, I forgot to add that one of the directors of this American company is Diane's ex-husband, in fact it seems that he's the one who's leading the takeover bid. Apparently, with him being one of the world's richest men, the divorce was quite the three-ring circus and it quickly became very acrimonious.'

Andy smiled, 'Now that makes much more sense. Getting even with your ex-wife, now that's grounds for murder alright.'

Chapter Thirteen

'So, do we have any suggestions as to what our next steps should be?' Andy asked.

'I think that we could go and see my contact at the FT,' Mac suggested. 'I think a chat with someone like him might shed a little more light on the case.'

'Good call, Mac. Can you ask him if we could speak to him this afternoon?' Andy asked.

'Sure.'

Mac got up and walked a few feet away while he made the call. His contact told him that he'd be free in a couple of hours.

'Do you think that this could be the lead we've been looking for?' Andy asked when Mac had finished his call.

'Love and money, they can be a lethal mixture, can't they?' Mac said. 'I have to admit that it looks promising and anyway if it's not murder then it's at least a case of blackmail, isn't it?'

'Come on then, let's get going,' Andy said as he stood up. 'If there's any traffic it could easily take us two hours to get into Central London. Toni and Leigh, can I ask you to carry on interviewing the Society's members? I'll give you a ring when we get back.'

It being London there was traffic and they arrived with only a minute or two to spare. They were lucky to get a disabled parking space opposite the black glass cube of the Financial Times building. Mac's contact, a short fat man with a receding hairline, was waiting for them in the lobby. After signing them in, he led them down a corridor and into a large meeting room. A man was already in the room and he was tucking into a tray of Krispy Kreme doughnuts.

Mac introduced his contact.

'Andy, this is Matt Loffkiss who is…what are you now, Matt?'

'I'm an Assistant Editor now Mac. This is Denzel Jordan,' Matt said as he gestured towards the doughnut eater. 'He's done some articles on Alix Stefanovic.'

Denzel was in his early thirties, wore jeans and a crumpled check shirt, but, like Matt, he had had a receding hairline and wore rimless glasses.

Mac introduced Andy. They sat down and helped themselves to a coffee each.

'Sorry,' Denzel apologised in an American accent as he grabbed another doughnut. 'I haven't had anything since breakfast and I'm starving.'

'So, what's got the police so interested in AMMI and Alix Stefanovic? Is there a story in it for us?' Matt asked.

'There might be but I'm afraid I'm going to have to ask you to keep this under your hat for now. We're more interested in his ex-wife at the moment but we'd like to find out a bit more about him too. Tell us what you know,' Mac asked.

'It's a classic rags to riches tale,' Matt replied. 'He started out as a messenger boy on Wall Street and was found using one of their computers after hours to buy and sell shares. The story is that they were a millimetre away from calling the police when one of the product managers took a look at his trades. He was doing far better than they were so they gave him a job instead. Within six years he was running the business.'

'He's good at what he does then?' Andy asked.

'No,' Denzel said, taking another mouthful of doughnut. 'He's bloody magnificent at what he does. Of course, there's some talk about how his trades are now self-fulfilling prophecies, if he buys then everyone wants to buy as well. Even so, I'd still say that he's got one of the best financial brains in the world.'

Matt nodded his agreement.

'You sound as if you admired him,' Mac stated.

'I suppose I do in a way,' Denzel confirmed as another doughnut bit the dust. 'He makes things happen and not always in the way you might think. He's a very creative guy.'

'What about his ex-wife?' Andy asked.

'Ah, now that was a story,' Matt said with a smile. 'God but it was great copy for a while, one of the richest and most powerful men in the world getting skewered by his ex-wife. It was a journalist's dream really.'

'She took him to the bloody cleaners,' Denzel confirmed.

'How much did she get?' Mac asked.

'Sixty five point five million dollars,' Matt replied.

'I suppose that in their circles that's not so much,' Mac said.

'That's sixty five point five million dollars a year,' Denzel pointed out.

'A year!' Andy said with some disbelief.

'Plus a hundred and ninety million up front,' Matt said. 'Mind you he could afford it. It would be like me paying a parking fine I'd guess but that wasn't the best part. After dragging him through the courts, washing all their dirty laundry in public and getting one of the biggest alimony pay-outs in history what does she do?'

He paused for effect.

'She had a private hearing after the judgement and made it clear that she wouldn't soil herself by taking a penny of his money. She turned it all down. Now there's a woman with balls of steel!'

'Wow, he must have really upset her. How did he react?' Andy asked.

'You think he'd be happy at not having to part with all that money but instead he went totally apeshit for a while,' Denzel said. 'I heard he was nearly done for assault after going on a massive binge and beating up some guy in a bar who was taking the piss. Of course, his people managed to hush it all up by the liberal application of his cheque book.'

Matt seamlessly continued, 'And, in one of those drunken episodes he was heard to say that he'd get even with his wife if it killed him. 'That English bitch' he called her.'

'What's the story behind the takeover? It sounds to me as if the motive behind it could be more personal than business?' Mac asked.

'I'd guess that it's one hundred per cent personal. I mean 3C's not a bad target for AMMI but they're paying way above what you'd expect,' Matt said.

'Not only that,' Denzel continued, 'but why is Alix here in London running the whole show himself? That's not his normal style, he usually likes to pull the strings from afar and stay out of the limelight.'

'Alix Stefanovic is here in London?' Andy said with some surprise. 'Have you any idea how we can contact him?'

'Well, he wouldn't hand out his personal phone number to the likes of us now, would he?' Denzel said. He turned to look at his colleague. 'But there is someone who'd know, isn't there Matt?'

'His ex-wife would know the number. Alix is staying at the flat they used to live in. I think he's spent more time there over the last month than he ever did when they were married.'

Chapter Fourteen

They drove through a part of London that Mac had once worked in when he'd first joined the Met. It was right on the river and back then had been a dirty, run-down industrial area at the heart of which an old gin distillery had stood. It was all very different and very up-market now.

They pulled up outside a tall glittering block of flats overlooking the river. A man immaculately dressed in tails and a top hat gave them a sour look. Andy flashed his warrant card and said he had an appointment with Alix Stefanovic.

'Yes,' the man said as he looked them up and down with clear disapproval.

He led them through a plush lobby and into a mirrored lift. He inserted a key and selected the top floor. The lift was so smooth that Mac wasn't even sure it was moving. The doors opened and he gestured at them to leave the lift.

'Which flat does Mr. Stefanovic live in?' Andy reasonably asked.

The man's face showed his utter disdain.

'There is only one residence on this floor, through the double doors there.' He pointed. 'Ask Mr. Stefanovic to ring the lobby when you're ready to leave.'

The lift doors silently closed behind them.

The door opened and a man dressed in a white shirt and jeans appeared. The shirt was silk and the jeans had a designer label on and were obviously made to measure.

'You're the police?'

Andy showed him his warrant card.

'Please come in.'

The man was slim and in his late thirties although his hair was already starting to grey at the sides. Mac thought that he was striking rather than good looking but the thing that struck him most was the air of sure authority he emanated.

'Can I get you anything?' he asked, as he gestured towards a long white leather sofa which stood in the centre of an enormous room.

Behind him the whole wall was comprised of what looked like one massive sheet of glass. The sun had come out and the view over the Thames was truly magnificent.

'No thanks,' Andy replied as they all sat down. 'We're looking into the death of Mrs. Catherine Gascoigne.'

'I figured this had something to do with my wife, well ex-wife, as you contacted me on my personal number but Catherine Gascoigne?'

He gave it a few seconds thought.

'There's a Gascoigne on the 3C shareholder list. Is that the same one?'

'Yes, it is,' Andy replied. 'She was found dead some days ago and the cause of death was thallium.'

This really seemed to surprise the billionaire.

'Thallium? That's really strange.' He leant forward. 'Do you suspect Diane of having something to do with this murder?'

Mac thought he was either very quick or the one behind the blackmail attempt.

'She's a suspect but just one of many at the moment,' Andy said. 'This is the real reason for our visit.'

Andy started the video off and passed over his phone.

'This was sent to your ex-wife by someone calling themselves '3C or not 3C' urging her to sell her shares.'

Mac watched Alix Stefanovic intently. His face gave little away. Alix Stefanovic returned the phone to Andy and then stood up. He turned his back and looked out at the view over the river.

'Did this video come from someone in your company?' Andy asked.

He turned and said, 'Almost definitely. Has Diane made a formal complaint?'

'No, not yet.'

'If she does let me know. I'll make sure that we turn over all the evidence we can lay my hands on.'

'And if she doesn't?' Mac asked.

'I've got a good idea who it might be but, knowing them, it might be hard to prove even in a court of law. However, I don't need a court. We have interests all over the world that need looking after. This person', he said the word with real distaste, 'and anyone else involved will shortly find themselves representing our interests in Siberia and for quite some time to come. I have to ask you gentlemen to believe me when I say that I never meant for this to happen, someone's really overstepped the mark. She must think...' he left the sentence dangling.

For a fleeting second Mac thought he saw a flash of real sadness in Alix's face and he had an idea.

'Why are you really trying to take over 3C?' Mac asked. 'All the world thinks you're getting even with your ex-wife by attempting to buy and then destroy the company her father built up from nothing. She believes that's the case too. Is that what this takeover's about or are you really just trying to get your ex-wife's attention?'

The billionaire looked up at Mac with a tinge of admiration.

'You're quick Mr. Maguire which is only what I would have expected from a former Detective Chief Super-intendent with your reputation. When I married Diane, I had an ego as big as the world. I was so sure that I could have everything, I could have Diane and I could still have her friend Claudia.

It was Claudia who introduced us in the first place and I think she was quite jealous when I fell for Diane and we got married. However, she soon seemed to settle quite happily for the role of mistress. I figured that, even if Diane found out, she'd probably just ignore it. After all being married to one of the world's richest men is something to aspire to and a little thing like an affair can be overlooked in that case, can't it? I mean you'd have to be mad to give all that money up or so I thought then. So, when she found out I'd been cheating on her, I made my mind up to go out and buy her something really nice and I figured that would be the end of it. Boy was I wrong. When I got home that evening, I found the crotches had been cut out of all my trousers and all my watches had been seen to with the heel of her shoe. The rest of my stuff had disappeared too. According to our friendly doorman she got a local homeless charity in to clear the flat. To think that there's some guy walking out there sleeping rough in a pair of ten thousand dollar shoes.

Anyway, I figured that, as everyone has a game plan, then it must be the alimony that she was really after. I was absolutely sure of it when she got the hearing in the States and managed to get the number one divorce attorney on her team. I knew then that I was screwed but I thought, well that's the price you pay. In my infinite arrogance I was wrong yet again and, ask anyone, I'm never wrong. She used every bit of her ingenuity to get the maximum pay-out and then threw the money back in my face.

I realised much too late that there were only two women in the world who I could be sure had loved me for myself, my mother and Diane. I've tried every way I can think of to contact her, I've sent flowers and gifts, all returned. I turned up at events she was supposed to be attending but she somehow always got wind and was gone before I got there. I sat on her doorstep once all night in the freezing cold and she wouldn't even open the door. I've even had one of those planes trailing a message buzz her house. So, I figured that she'd have to see me if I staged a takeover of her beloved 3C but no, she's still successfully dodging me at every turn. I'd give just about anything for ten minutes with her.'

The room was silent for a moment then Andy asked, 'Is there anything else you can tell us that might help us with the murder?'

'Just that it wasn't Diane. If she was the sort of woman who could find it in her heart to murder someone, believe me, I'd be dead meat right now.'

Andy stood up and held his hand out.

'Thank you for your time.'

Alix walked them to the lift. The lift door opened revealing the man in the top hat.

'Can I ask you to do me a big favour?' he asked.

'If we can,' Andy replied.

'If you're going to see Diane can you tell her I'll be in Tony's restaurant from eight tomorrow evening? Tell her that, if she gives me half an hour, I'll drop the takeover.'

'And if she doesn't?' Mac asked.

'Tell her I'll drop the takeover anyway and I'll stop trying to contact her.'

Mac nodded. Alix stood there as the lift doors closed. He thought that Alix Stefanovic, for all his money, was probably a bit of a sad case too.

As they made their way back through the inevitable traffic jams Andy and Mac discussed the next steps the investigation might take. Andy wanted to keep working his way through the membership list so Mac volunteered to see Diane and give her the message. He also said, while he was in the area, he'd drop in at the restaurant and see if he could get a copy of the CCTV images for the evening before Catherine Gascoigne was found dead. It had been another long day and he was starting to feel the strain a bit. He rang Tim and postponed the pub again.

They were just nearing Stevenage when Andy's phone rang. He pulled off the motorway and parked as soon as he could. It was a video message.

'Now that's really interesting,' Andy said.

'What is it?' Mac asked.

'It's from Alix Stefanovic. It's the video of Diane Caversham going to Catherine's house,' Andy explained, 'but this version's a bit longer. We see Diane knocking at Catherine's door and waiting. Eventually she gives up and walks back past the pub and into the car park. She then gets into the Ferrari and drives off in the direction of her house.'

He started the video off again and passed the phone to Mac.

'So, rather than it being evidence proving that she might have carried out the murder, it really supports the case that she's innocent, doesn't it?' Andy stated.

'That's right,' Mac replied. 'Of course, she could have always come back later and done the deed but she couldn't have used the Ferrari, it's far too noisy.'

'So, we're back at square one, aren't we?' Andy said looking a little dejected.

'Something will turn up,' Mac predicted cheerily although he had no idea what that something might be.

Leigh was waiting for him at the station.

'What was he like?' she asked as they walked towards the car park at the police station. 'I've never met a billionaire before.'

'Have you ever read Pride and Prejudice by any chance?' Mac asked.

'No, but I saw the film.'

'Well, he's pretty much Darcy to a tee. Good looking, very rich and very proud. I think there's a good chance that he still loves his ex-wife too. He's definitely pissed his Elizabeth off but can he get her back again like in the book?'

He looked at his watch. It was only seven o'clock.

'Are you doing anything right now?'

'No, why?' she answered.

'I was just wondering if we could visit Diane and the pub this evening?'

He was also thinking that he might benefit from having a little blue pill and a lie in tomorrow.

'That's okay with me,' Leigh said. 'I've only got some unpacked boxes waiting for me at home.'

The Ferrari was parked outside so Mac was fairly sure that Diane must be in. He rang the bell and she opened the door. She looked very elegant in a long black gown and high heels.

'I'm sorry, were you going out?' Mac asked.

'I've been invited somewhere but I'm not sure I want to go if I'm being honest. Please come in.'

Once they'd sat down, she said, 'I take it that you've seen him.'

She emphasised the 'him' with a look of distaste.

'Yes, we did and thanks very much for letting us have his number,' Mac said. 'We had a very interesting conversation.'

'I'll bet you did. Did he admit to being behind the video?' she asked.

'No, but he said he had an idea who was.'

'Of course, he'd never get his own hands dirty,' she said acidly.

'I don't think it's like that. I don't think he meant that to happen.'

Diane looked puzzled.

'What do you mean?'

'Well, he's sent us a longer version which shows you walking away from Catherine's and getting into your car and driving off. He said that, if you want to press charges, then he'll provide all the evidence he can.'

'And if I don't press charges?' Diane asked.

'He said that he has some business interests in Siberia and that whoever was behind the blackmail attempt will find themselves representing him there for quite a few years to come,' Mac replied.

She said nothing.

'Is it true that you've refused to see him since the divorce?' Mac asked.

'Why would I want to see that bastard's face again?'

'I think that he's just trying to get your attention, that's what the takeover bid was all about, a chance to meet you.'

'And you believe him?' she asked.

'I do.' Mac said. 'He said something interesting, he said he'd found out too late that the only women in the world that he was absolutely sure that loved him for himself were his mother and you.'

She stood up and started pacing up and down.

'It's true,' she said. 'I did love him...then.'

'He said he'd be in Tony's restaurant tomorrow at eight and, if you give him half an hour, he'll drop the takeover.'

'I thought he was still angry at me, wanting to get even.' She was thoughtful for a moment. 'And if I don't turn up?' she asked.

'He said he'll drop the takeover anyway. He also said he'll stop trying.'

This seemed to disturb her for some reason.

'He said that he'll stop trying, really?'

'That's what he said.'

She sat down and held her head in her hands.

'God, I so wish that daddy was still alive, that he could tell me what to do. I suppose that's why I came here when we split up. This was his house, his little hide-away, it's where he did his best thinking he always said. The problem is I just can't seem to think at all at the moment.'

'Well, he would have clearly seen that it was making you utterly miserable,' Mac said. 'Perhaps he might have said that it doesn't have to be this way, sometimes you have to give people a second chance in life.'

'You do?' she said looking unconvinced.

'We all make mistakes, don't we?' Mac said. 'After all Elizabeth forgave Darcy in the end, didn't she?'

'Yes, she did,' Diane said, brightening up a little.

'It was quite a lot to forgive too, wasn't it?' Mac asked.

'Yes, yes I suppose it was. Thank you,' she said giving them the faintest of smiles.

Mac thought that Diane definitely looked a little more cheerful when they left her. He just hoped that he'd done the right thing.

Outside Leigh asked, 'Exactly what was it that Elizabeth forgave Darcy for? I must have been making tea during that bit.'

'Elizabeth's sister Jane was in love with Darcy's friend Mr. Bingley. However, Darcy persuaded his friend that Elizabeth's sister wasn't a good enough match for him. When Jane went to London to try and see Bingley, Darcy made sure that she'd fail. This made Jane absolutely miserable. So, Elizabeth was seething when she found out that it was Darcy who had engineered it all and that he was responsible for keeping Jane and Mr. Bingley apart. So, when Darcy asked Elizabeth to marry him, she turned him down flat. She said that 'had you behaved in a more gentleman-like manner...' In those days that was probably the nearest thing to using a swear word.'

As they drove down the road to the Earl Lewin Mac wondered how it would all turn out. It was now half past seven and the pub was heaving. They made their way past the queue and Mac managed to get Nico's attention.

'Is your boss around?' Mac asked.

'It's his day off,' Nico replied. 'But he lives over the shop as it were. Come on I'll take you up to him.'

They went through a door marked private and up a narrow flight of stairs which Mac took very carefully as there was no bannister. He led Mac and Leigh into a spacious room, a sort of very large bedsit dominated by a state of the art kitchen in one corner. Simon Gent was cooking something and the aroma was entirely wonderful. Mac suddenly realised that he was very hungry.

'Mr. Maguire and his lovely assistant. I hope you're both hungry,' Simon Gent said.

'I am that,' Mac replied sincerely.

'Good sit down at the table there and I'll bring it over in a minute. It's just a little experiment but I always end up doing loads more than I should so I'm really glad that you've both come.'

Mac sat down. If the food was as good as its aroma suggested then he knew he was in for a rare treat.

As he brought two plates to the table Simon asked, 'I take it that you're Irish with a name like Maguire?'

'Yes, I was born there and came over here when I was young.'

'I hope you like white pudding then?'

'I love it,' Mac replied with complete sincerity.

Simon brought a large frying pan over to the table.

'Good, I'd like your opinion on this. It's Irish Bream with a White Pudding and Carrageen Moss crust served with warm soda bread. I'm thinking of doing a special for St. Patricks Day.'

It looked beautiful. Mac took a corner off the fish with his fork and put it in his mouth. It was absolutely totally magnificent.

'I've just died and gone to heaven,' he said as he continued eating.

Simon smiled broadly but Mac noticed that he was looking mostly at Leigh.

'I'll take that as a yes then,' the chef said.

Mac didn't say another word until he'd wiped the plate clean with the bread.

'You're a very talented man,' Mac said.

'That was fantastic,' Leigh said, handing the chef her empty plate.

'Thanks, it'll be on the menu then.'

The chef cleared the table and then sat down with them.

'So, how can I help the police?' he asked.

Mac had almost forgotten why he'd come.

'I saw some CCTV cameras downstairs, one on the front entrance and another one on the car park. I wondered if you keep the images?'

'I was just looking at some of them before I started cooking. Here.'

Mac and Leigh followed him to the far corner of the room where a very large TV hung on the wall. Simon picked up the remote control and Mac saw people opening the pub door and leaving.

'I'm not interested in the car park stuff just these,' the chef explained.

'Why?' Mac asked.

'It's something that I learned from one of the first chefs I worked for. He always used to look at the videos of the customers as they left. He used to say that people may smile and say everything was okay and wonderful but, when they step out of the restaurant, you'll see the truth on their faces. Do they still look happy or do they look pissed off? He always said that the mask dropped when they were leaving. I've found it very useful especially for my regulars. If they don't look happy when they leave, then I try and find out why.'

'I'm quite amazed at your attention to detail,' Mac said. 'I've no doubt you'll go far but to get back to the case, have you any images for the night before Catherine Gascoigne was murdered?'

'Sure, I think they go back a year or more. What was the date?'

Mac told him and he got the relevant video up in less than a minute.

'What time approximately?' the chef asked.

'Around nine-thirty in the evening.'

He quickly found the image of Diane leaving the pub.

'Can we switch to the car park?' Mac asked.

Simon did so and seven minutes later they saw Diane walk past the camera and disappear to the left, re-appearing a minute or so later behind the wheel of the Ferrari. She then drove out of Willian towards her home.

'Thanks Simon,' Mac said. 'I think that's all I need to see for now. Is there any chance that you could email that video to this address?'

He gave Simon Andy's email address and thanked him again for the wonderful meal. Leigh followed him out a minute or so later looking a bit flustered.

Nico showed them out. As he held open the door Mac gestured for him to follow him outside.

'Nico, I know all about you and Catherine,' Mac said. 'Why didn't you tell me when I was here before?'

He looked like a kid who'd been caught with his hand in the cookie jar.

'I'm sorry Mr. Maguire but I didn't want to talk about it in there. I didn't want anyone to overhear. I've got a wife and kids.'

Mac let it go at that.

'Tell me everything you know about Catherine and I mean everything.'

'Okay, we used to meet at her house every Tuesday and Friday after she'd eaten at the restaurant. She'd go back and get herself ready while I was closing up here.'

'And she paid you for these visits?'

The waiter nodded.

'But it wasn't like that, well not after I'd known her a while. We became friends. I really liked her Mr. Maguire.

141

I know she was in her forties but she looked after herself. I thought she was quite beautiful.'

'Was it during one of these visits when she told you about the book offer?' Mac asked.

'Yes, we'd have a drink afterwards and have a chat before I went home. She was very excited about the book. It was a fantastic chance for her to get better known.'

'Did you discuss anything else that might be of help?'

Nico gave it some thought.

'Yes, there was something but I'm not sure...'

'Tell us anyway,' Mac said.

'Okay, I think it was around three weeks or so ago on a Friday night and it happened when she was crossing the road just there.'

He pointed to a spot about twenty yards down the road.

'As she was crossing a car came straight at her. She thought that she was going to get run over but the car swerved at the very last minute and just avoided her. She said that it went up the kerb and onto the pavement before driving off. The car didn't have its lights on so Catherine reckoned that it was just someone from the pub who'd had too much to drink.'

Mac wasn't so sure.

'Did she notice anything about the car that might help us to identify it?'

'Not really, she said it was dark coloured but she didn't know much about cars.'

'It definitely wasn't a sports car then?' Mac asked.

Nico gave Mac a sharp look.

'You mean like Diane's car? No, Catherine knew that car well enough. I think it must have been some sort of saloon. 'Just a normal car' were the words she used.'

'Did she ever mention getting any threatening letters?'

'No. Why did she get some?' Nico asked looking puzzled.

Mac didn't answer.

'You know I'm still wondering about you and Catherine and Diane. I mean Diane's a really good-looking woman and quite young, so how come you preferred Catherine's company?'

Nico shrugged.

'Yes, Diane is beautiful but what's that song? Yes 'beautiful but oh so boring' well that was Diane.'

'Boring, in what way?'

'Well, I'll be honest, I really like sex but with Diane it was sometimes like being in a sweet shop and then being told that you're not allowed to touch anything.'

Mac was surprised.

'Oh, we had sex sometimes,' Nico continued, 'but more often than not we'd just lie on the bed fully clothed, she'd have her back to me and I'd hug her until she fell asleep. Now Catherine was totally different, the minute we went through her front door it was clothes off and sex, sex, sex. God, I'll really miss her.'

'Is there anything you can think of that you haven't told us already?' Mac asked.

'I'm sorry no.'

Mac gave him his number in case he remembered anything else.

As they seated themselves in the car Mac found he was curious and asked Leigh a question.

'Why were you looking so flustered back then, when we left Simon Gent?'

She had a big grin on her face as she held out her hand.

'He kissed it!' she said. 'He kissed my hand.'

It was the happiest Mac had seen her.

Leigh drove him home. It had been quite a day. He sat on the settee thinking things over when he suddenly became aware of how tired and how close to melt-down he was. He got undressed, took a blue pill and got straight into bed. He fell asleep almost immediately.

...and another poisoning

It was just getting too delicious.

Even walking along the street, he would cast his eye over neighbours and acquaintances and wonder, 'Are you going to be next?' This thought always made him smile. People had told him many times that he was looking much happier these days. If only they knew why.

He had expanded his operations and enjoyed some nice days out in places he'd never been to before. However, his next project was somewhat closer to home. He'd rid the world of quite a few slugs by now. So many, in fact, that he decided that he'd earned a little bonus and that bonus was Matthew Silsoe.

He liked his work. His work was all about numbers and he liked numbers. They were honest and reliable. Two and two always made four, they always did and they always would. His work was recognised within the company. They used him to train others and to write procedures. He'd been offered managerial positions on more than one occasion but he had turned them all down. With a person two and two might make four one day then five the next and absolutely anything at all on yet another day. People were inherently unreliable.

Matthew Silsoe hadn't been on his radar until one day when he overheard a conversation. He'd been in the cubicle doing the Times crossword when two men came into the toilets to use the urinals. One of them was Silsoe.

'Between you and me Old Derrington's retiring and I've been given the nod that I'm going to be taking over,' Silsoe said with more than a hit of triumphalism. 'The first thing that I'm going to do is sack that odd little number cruncher. I know he's good at what he does but I must say that I can't stand the chap. Anyway, he's not exactly very dynamic, is he? Once I get myself behind

Derrington's desk he'll be straight out of the door and I'll get someone younger in.'

It didn't take him long to figure out that the 'odd little number cruncher' Silsoe was referring to must be himself. David Derrington, his boss for many years, had always appreciated him and had just let him get on with the job. Now he was retiring. He had no idea what he'd done to upset Silsoe and, if he was being honest, he didn't much care. Within a minute of hearing the conversation he'd already started formulating his plan.

A number of his colleagues went for a drink most Fridays before going home for the weekend. He sometimes joined them before catching his train so no-one was surprised when he turned up on that particular Friday evening. He bought Silsoe a drink and they had a chat. He told him that he'd heard that he was up for Derrington's job and wished him luck. Of course, Silsoe accepted the drink. He thought he was being buttered up when in fact he'd just had his death sentence delivered to him. The nice big glass of juicy red wine that he was knocking back had quite a wallop and all supplied by the wonderful Mr. T.

Silsoe was in a good mood that night and had quite a few drinks as everyone there told the police afterwards. After all he was celebrating his imminent promotion and a big pay rise.

The policemen nodded. They were now sure that they'd found the reason for his death.

Silsoe always caught the Northern Line home and he had the habit of standing near the tube tunnel at King's Cross station so he could get into one of the last two train carriages. This left him right opposite the station exit when he got off at his stop. While he was standing there, he suddenly felt nauseous. However, it was the sudden feeling that he was standing on red hot coals that made him lose his balance. He fell onto the track just as the train came out of the tunnel. There was nothing the driver could do. The cause of death was obvious and no-one looked any further.

When he first heard the terrible news, he shook his head, bemoaned the loss of an esteemed colleague and cried crocodile tears along with the rest of them.

Even when he was by the graveside and a certain thought struck him, his mournful expression remained intact. Poor Silsoe had apparently been neatly cut into two pieces by the train wheels, sliced apart just below the hips. He laughed inside as he remembered the very last words that he'd heard him speak.

'I'd better go home,' Silsoe had said, 'I think I'm getting a bit legless.'

Chapter Fifteen

Thursday

Leigh picked him up at ten thirty allowing Mac to have the luxury of a lie in. She'd already been to the station and had talked with Andy. He wanted them to try and interview the last two members of Anne's group and then meet him back at the station to discuss next steps.

'So how are you today?' she asked. 'You looked absolutely exhausted last night.'

Mac looked at her before he spoke. He could still detect a little smile and there was a lightness about her that he hadn't seen before. He thought that she should get her hand kissed more often.

'I'm really sorry about that,' he said. 'I don't know whether it's the drugs or my condition but I sometimes get these bouts of exhaustion. I'm fine now I've had a nice long sleep. Anyway, what's next?'

'Andy wants us to visit the last two members of Anne's group and then report back to him.'

'Okay, so let's try this Zsuzsanna Dixon first as we know where she works,' Mac suggested.

St. Hilda's School was a private school, girls only. It had a good reputation and charged a good price for it. Leigh drove into the car park. The school consisted mainly of a large Edwardian pile attempting to look like a grand country mansion and pretty much succeeding. A nice lady in the lobby took them down several corridors, their footsteps echoing as the upper half of the walls were painted and the lower half tiled. She took them to a door that had a sign 'Mrs. Z. Dixon, Deputy Head'. She opened the door for them and went back to her duties.

A small long faced lady in her fifties with a severe bun and wire rimmed spectacles stood up behind the desk.

'I've been expecting you,' she stated as she held her hand out.

Mac introduced himself and Leigh.

'Why were you expecting us exactly?' Mac asked.

'I've heard that you've already spoken to Anne and the rest of our group so I knew you'd be getting around to me sooner or later.'

'Well, not quite everyone. We're having some problems tracking down Peggy Corning. Do you have any idea where she lives?' Mac asked.

Zsuzsanna gave it some thought.

'No, I'm sorry I don't but it can't be far from here. I met her once as we were both walking to meet Anne at the library and she said it had taken her twenty minutes or so to walk there.'

'Do you have her email address?' Mac asked.

'Yes, I've got the emails of everyone in our group.'

'Can you do me a favour then and email her? Ask her if she can ring this number.'

Mac gave her his mobile number. He waited while she did this.

'So, what can you tell us about Catherine Gascoigne?' Mac asked.

'Not much that you haven't heard already I'd dare say. Catherine and I weren't exactly close friends.'

'I take it that you were once a member of the Society?'

'Yes, I was one of the founding members along with Catherine, Olivia and Penny.'

'So, you were friends with her at one time?' Mac asked.

'Not really, I was one of Penny's friends. I never liked Catherine that much.'

'So why did you leave?'

'Why did anyone leave the Society?' Zsuzsanna said. 'It was Catherine of course. She could be so single minded about things that she'd often run rough shod over anyone who disagreed with her. I stuck it out because I loved the books and the company but, when Anne started her own group up, I was more than glad to 'decamp to the enemy' as Catherine once put it. It was the best thing that I ever did.'

Mac gave this some thought.

'I take it that you have chemistry labs in the school?'

'We do,' she confirmed with a little smile, 'but we don't keep Thallium there if that's what you're thinking. Something like that would be far too toxic for our girls to be messing about with.'

This was only as Mac had been expecting. He felt that he was getting nowhere so he decided to cut to the chase.

'Mrs. Dixon did you kill Catherine Gascoigne?'

There was a moment of hesitation which really interested Mac.

'Mr. Maguire, it wasn't me who killed her,' Zsuzsanna replied with a shake of her head.

'But you're not sorry she's dead?'

'No, I'm not,' she said with feeling, 'but I'm far from alone in that from what I've heard.'

'When did you find out that Catherine was dead?'

'Not until Tuesday morning when I opened Anne's email.'

'When was the email sent?' Mac asked.

'On Monday, I think, but it was my day off on Monday and I was working on something.'

'So, you don't look at your emails when you're working?' Mac asked.

'Oh no, it's far too much of a distraction,' she replied. 'I turn my phone off too. I was doing some research into Jane's early attempts at writing and how they might have had an effect on her later novels. I'd been at it all weekend and I'd printed off quite a lot of material. As I had Monday off and felt I was on to something I kept at it, going through everything and making notes.'

'Have you anything else to add?' Mac asked.

'I'm sorry but I'm sure that whatever I know about Catherine you'll have heard several times before. As I've said we were far from being close.'

There was a question that Mac wanted to ask.

'Your name, Zsuzsanna, that's unusual. Where did your family originally come from?'

'From Hungary, Mr. Maguire. My family came over to England not long after the uprising in nineteen fifty six. Before I married my husband, my name was Zsuzsanna Karoly.'

'Is your husband still around?'

Her face told him he wasn't.

'No, unfortunately he died four years ago.'

He thanked her and gave her his number in case she thought of anything else.

As they walked back along the echoing corridor Leigh asked, 'So what do you think? Could she have done it?'

'I'm not sure but I noticed some hesitation when I asked her that,' Mac replied. 'The problem at the moment is the apparent lack of motive but I'm fairly sure that there's something that she's keeping to herself. I think that we might need to do a bit more digging on Mrs. Dixon.'

In the car park Mac noticed that the staff parking spaces had their names on little plates screwed to the wall. He looked for Mrs. Dixon's. It was a dark blue Vauxhall and far from new. He looked at the driver's side wheel and body work but found nothing suspicious.

'Leigh, when we get back to the station can you ask if someone can call all the tyre repair centres in the area to see if anyone's turned up with a damaged tyre or wheel on the driver's side? If they went up the kerb at speed then they must have done some damage.'

'Sure,' Leigh replied. 'Are you thinking that it might have been a serious murder attempt after all?'

'You never know,' Mac replied. 'If it was an attempt at a hit and run murder then it looks like the driver lost their nerve at the last second. Perhaps poison was an easier way for them, who knows? Anyway, it would be nice to rule it out one way or the other.'

As they drove towards the station Leigh said, 'You asking her about when she knew that Catherine was dead. Why was that important?'

Mac frowned.

'It's that letter we found. Like the potential hit and run it bothers me.'

'Do you think that the murderer sent it?'

'No and that's why I'd like to find out who did. It would at least rule out another suspect.'

Leigh gave Mac a puzzled look.

'How come?' she asked.

'It was definitely put in the letter box after Catherine had been found dead, sometime during the night as I'd guess that it's not something you'd want to be spotted delivering. Whoever killed Catherine knew that she was dead as did Penny, Olivia and probably quite a few others by then but I'd bet that whoever was responsible for that letter didn't.'

'And Mrs. Dixon, with her phone off and not having checked her emails, definitely wouldn't have known,' Leigh said. 'But, if it was her, wouldn't she have noticed the police having been around and the crime scene tape across the door?'

'Not necessarily. I'd bet that letter was literally put in the letter box in the middle of the night to minimise the chances of being seen. Drive slowly up towards the box, toss the letter in and quickly drive off. They probably wouldn't have noticed anything as the house is well back from the road.'

Leigh gave it some thought as she drove back to the station.

At the briefing Andy revealed that he and Toni had turned up little of interest.

'We've still got quite a few members to get through so we might as well keep going on that and hope something turns up,' he said looking a little dejected.

Mac was quiet for a moment.

'Do you mind if I stay here and do some research?' he asked. 'There's something I want to check up on.'

Andy was more than happy. If Mac had a lead, he was all for him following it up. Andy gave Toni and Leigh a list each. He'd decided they'd be better splitting up to try and get through as many members as possible. Mac was surprised at Andy letting Leigh out on her own but then he had a sudden thought. It was a thought that might explain a lot.

He spent the next four hours glued to a computer screen. For three of those he found nothing but then he hit gold dust. He kept digging and found even more.

He was eventually interrupted by a young detective.

'Mr. Maguire, DI Reid said to give this straight to you if he wasn't around. He said you might find it of interest.'

It was a list of car registrations that had recently had some work done on the driver's side tyre or wheel. A registration number leapt out of him. After all he'd seen it not that long ago.

Things were suddenly getting very interesting indeed.

Chapter Sixteen

Andy seemed to think that it was very interesting too. He was more than happy for Mac and Leigh to follow it up. He and Toni would carry on working through the still lengthy list of members.

Mac decided that his first call should be on Anne Holding. Unfortunately, the library was closed so he had to find her home address. It turned out that she lived in a nice semi-detached house just off Pixmore Way.

She smiled when she saw who was calling. However, when Mac started talking about Zsuzsanna Dixon he noticed that the smile quickly disappeared. She definitely knew something.

'She's been through a bit of a bad time,' Anne explained. 'She lost her husband a few years ago then a year later she got passed over again as headmistress. They'd been promising her the position for ages and she's worked so hard for that school. They needed someone younger they said, someone with more energy. Even if that was true, I still wonder why they couldn't they have said it a little less hurtfully.'

'Tell me about the plagiarism.'

'The plagiarism?' Anne said with some surprise.

'Catherine stole one of Zsuzsanna's ideas, didn't she?'

'Yes, but how on earth did you find that out?' Anne asked. 'I thought that I was the only one she'd talked to about that.'

'It wasn't too hard,' Mac replied. 'I looked at Catherine's published works and, unlike all her earlier articles, one of the more recent papers was about something that Jane had written when she was young. As I knew that Zsuzsanna was an expert in the area and that Catherine had some previous when it came to plagiarism, it was easy to come to the conclusion that there might be something underhand going on.'

'Well you're spot on there,' Anne said. 'It wasn't just me after all, it turns out that Catherine was a serial plagiarist. I find it strange though as she had some good ideas of her own. I never figured out why she needed to steal other people's ideas too.'

'What happened with Zsuzsanna Dixon?' Mac asked.

'Well, Zsuzsanna's very clever and she works very hard at her research,' Anne replied. 'As you said, her speciality is Jane's early writings. Jane wrote from quite a young age and Zsuzsanna was especially interested in the bits of writing she did when she was a teenager. A while ago she uncovered something, a link between an early character and Elizabeth Bennett. The earlier character was called Eliza too. Anyway, she made the mistake of consulting Catherine to see what she thought of her discovery. Catherine persuaded her that it was only a minor point and that perhaps she should start looking at something more interesting. If only Zsuzsanna had a bit more confidence in her own abilities and had just gone ahead and published it anyway. Unfortunately for her though, she didn't. Instead she did as Catherine suggested and dropped the whole line of research. Anyway, the research proved so minor that some weeks later Catherine published a paper on it for the university.'

'How did Zsuzsanna take that?' Mac asked.

'She was very upset as you might guess. She might have been able to prove plagiarism too but she didn't want any fuss so she quietly resigned from the Society. She's kept any research she's done to herself ever since.'

'Did anything happen around three weeks ago that might have upset Zsuzsanna?' Mac asked.

Anne frowned.

'Yes, Catherine won an award for that particular piece of 'ground breaking' research. It even made the local papers.'

Mac thought that this might make excellent grounds for murder. The award would be just rubbing salt into an already open wound.

'Why didn't you tell me this earlier?' Mac asked.

Anne's frown deepened.

'I was hoping she'd tell you herself,' she replied. 'I like Zsuzsanna and I didn't want to be the one who got her in trouble. Some think she's a bit of a dry stick but there's more to her than that and she's been dealt such a bad hand recently. She's not a murderer, Mr. Maguire, of that I'm certain.'

He thanked Anne and left. He stood on the pavement thinking for a moment. He looked at his watch. It was five thirty.

'Have we got Mrs. Dixon's home address?' he asked.

It proved to be a little grander than Anne's semi. It was a large detached house near the Cloisters. The driveway was empty so Mac made no move to get out of the car.

'We might still be able to catch her at the school,' Leigh suggested.

Mac shook his head.

'I'd sooner we waited for her here. If we're seen talking to her twice in one day tongues will probably wag.'

'And you're worried about that?' Leigh asked.

'Well, I know she looks like a good suspect but I've still got some doubts. I'd bet she was behind the wheel when Catherine had her near miss and there's a good chance that she might also be behind the threatening letters but murder? If she really wanted to kill Catherine why not just run her over when she had the chance?'

A dark blue Vauxhall pulled into the driveway. Zsuzsanna had her key in the door when she spotted Mac and Leigh making their way towards her. He could tell from her expression that she knew that they knew.

'Can we talk inside, Mrs. Dixon?' Mac asked.

Once they'd seated themselves Mac simply said, 'Tell me everything and leave nothing out.'

Zsuzsanna's lower lip trembled as a single tear ran down her face.

'Oh God, how did I end up here?' she said. Her hands were visibly shaking. 'Not long ago I had a husband, job prospects and friends. Now, I've got nothing.'

'You've still got some friends,' Mac stated.

'Have I? I wonder how many I'll have after this gets out? Hate is such a terrible thing Mr. Maguire. It was as though Catherine was responsible for everything bad that's happened to me but that's really stupid, isn't it? I never thought of myself as being stupid before but recently I haven't been so sure.'

'Did you try to run Catherine down?'

She nodded.

'I wanted to kill her so badly or at least I thought I did at the time. It was the award that Catherine received. It was just the last straw for me somehow. I think it sent me quite mad for a while. I began watching her and I thought my best chance would be in the evening when she left the pub. So, one night I waited outside in my car with the engine running and the lights switched off. When I saw her crossing the road, I put my foot down and drove straight at her. Then she turned and looked at me as I came towards her. She was standing in a pool of light from a street lamp and I could clearly see her face. I could see fear there and, in that split second, I wondered what in God's name was I doing? I swerved around her and drove on. It was like a bad dream, I still can't quite believe it myself, that I would try and kill another human being. I was surprised that she didn't report it to the police. I've been waiting ages for a knock on the door.'

'She assumed that it was just a drunk coming from the pub,' Mac said. 'What about the letters?'

'I was mostly glad that I hadn't killed her but I was a bit disappointed in myself too if I'm honest. I forgot about killing her but I still felt the need to get back at her in some way and so I thought of the letters.'

'How many did you send?' Mac asked.

'Three in all.'

'You realise that the murder attempt and the letters make you an excellent suspect.'

Zsuzsanna sighed.

'When I heard that she might have already been dead when I posted the last letter, I'll be honest and admit that I panicked a bit. But then no-one came to see me for a while and I hoped that somehow you'd forgotten about me.'

'Is there anything else you can tell us?' Mac asked.

'I'm sorry no. I really have no idea who killed her.'

Mac stood up.

'I'll need you to come to the station with us and make a formal statement.'

'I take it that I'm being arrested then? And so, the whole mess will come out.'

She looked at Mac and Leigh despairingly.

'I'm afraid that might well be the case,' Mac said. 'However, it's not up to the police what happens, all we do is gather the evidence. The Crown Prosecution Service will decide whether to bring the matter to court or not.'

This didn't cheer her up any.

At the station Andy took her statement and then a police car drove Zsuzsanna Dixon home.

'So, what do you think will happen to her?' Mac asked.

'Well the CPS will have a look but I'd almost bet that they won't proceed with a charge. They always go on about having enough evidence to provide a realistic prospect of prosecution.'

'But she's admitted everything,' Leigh said, looking puzzled.

'The problem is that's all we've got. If she gets a good defence lawyer and they advise her to retract her statement then we might be lucky to get her for dangerous driving. All in all, I'll bet that the CPS will decide that it's more trouble than it's worth. You're sure that she didn't kill Catherine Gascoigne though?' Andy asked looking at Mac.

'She had her chance and she couldn't bring herself to do it,' Mac said. 'No, I don't think it's her.'

'So, another one who didn't kill Catherine that we can cross off the list. Just another eighty or ninety to go,' Andy said looking a bit down.

A few pints with Tim in the Magnets cheered Mac up. Yet it was all still on his mind when he went to bed that night. So much so that he forgot something very important.

Chapter Seventeen

Friday

The pain woke him up. It was dark so he turned on his reading lamp and glanced at the little alarm clock. It was only four o'clock. He sighed as he realised that he hadn't put on a new pain patch before going to bed. He knew there'd be no sleep for him until he changed his Fentanyl patch and allowed at least a couple of hours for it to kick in. At least he had something he could do in the meantime to take his mind off his discomfort.

He made himself a pot of coffee, switched the radio on and found a classical music station. He then opened the file on Philippa Hatch.

He looked at the photos from the suicide scene first. She'd hung herself from a light fitting in the hallway of a house. She still had her ball gown on. He could tell that the house was old, at least Victorian, from the height of the ceiling and the decorative mouldings. Some close-up shots showed that she'd simply looped a short length of electric cable around the bottom of the light fitting and then tied it around her neck. A kitchen chair lay on its side. Her feet were no more than a few inches off the floor. One shoe had fallen off and lay on its side. For some reason the shoe made it a much more poignant scene.

He'd seen quite a few suicides in his time, most of which had been by hanging. He'd seen quite a few failures too, usually because the light fittings hadn't been able to take the weight. He'd noticed that the fittings in some of the older houses seemed to be somewhat sturdier and that, plus the fact that she looked as if she didn't weigh much anyway, meant there would be no such reprieve for Miss Hatch.

One of the photos was of a sheet of paper that had been torn unevenly away from a notepad. In spidery handwriting it simply said, '*I've been lonely for far too long, PH*'.

Mac looked at this for quite a while.

He read the investigating officer's report twice. The investigation team seem to have been thorough and everything pointed to suicide. The Coroner's report also confirmed this. There was evidence given that about the time of her death she'd been depressed and her doctor had actually tried to get a bed for her in a local psychiatric hospital. Unfortunately, they were full. The Coroner's verdict was that 'Philippa Hatch killed herself while the balance of her mind was disturbed'.

Mac couldn't find any reason to disagree.

But why? The question mark he'd dreamed of flashed into his mind. For some reason he still felt that this might be the key to the whole case. She said in the note that she'd been lonely too long. What had been the tipping point that led her to commit suicide? Was it really something Catherine said or was it something else?

There were copies of statements from her neighbours. Although she'd lived in the same house for over forty years the statements were very short. All they seemed to know about Philippa was her name and that she lived very quietly. One said that she'd known Philippa's mother a little better as they'd gone to the same church. While being a devout Christian she was also described as being a hard woman who had shown no love for her daughter in public.

A name leapt out at Mac from another statement. It was from Anne Holding and in it she described the scene at the ball and how Catherine had upset Philippa.

The next statement was from Catherine herself. She said that Philippa had been a valuable member of the Letchworth Society of Janeites for a number of years. However, she'd seemed to be very upset on the night she took her life. Mac read the next part very carefully.

Catherine stated that, 'She was always a little up and down but she'd always been in good spirits for the balls before. However, that night I made a joke about pretending she was Miss Bates from Emma when she ran off in tears. I must admit that I hadn't noticed her getting upset. However, my friend Penny thought that it was something I said that seemed to have upset her, although neither of us could figure out what it might have been.'

Mac gave this some thought. He took his edition of Emma from the bookcase and read the passage where Miss Bates enters the ballroom. She is clearly excited at attending a ball and, in a breathless monologue lasting nearly two pages, she babbles on about many things including her mother. In fact, she mentions her quite a bit so he could understand why Catherine, addressing Philippa as Miss Bates, might have asked her about her mother. Mac had a sudden thought.

He read the investigating officer's report again. It referenced some related evidence but didn't say what it was. He looked at the clock. He was surprised to see that it was now seven o'clock. He carefully placed all the documents back into the file. He showered and shaved and thought. He now knew what he needed to do next and he found that he was eager to get on with it. After another quick cup of coffee and a couple of rounds of toast he set off.

He made a call as soon as he got to the station. They called him back a few minutes later with some good news. He rang Leigh and she said that she'd pick him up in five minutes. He left Andy a note explaining where he was going.

'So where are we off to so early in the day?' Leigh asked.

'To the Police Headquarters in Welwyn, they've got something for us to look at. By the way I re-read a bit of Jane Austen's 'Emma' this morning, about the ball at the

Crown, and it was very interesting. I was reading about a character in the book called Miss Bates...'

'Is this the same Miss Bates that Amanda mentioned?' Leigh asked.

'Yes, that's right, very well remembered.'

Leigh gave him a smile.

'Anyway, I was reading about Miss Bates,' Mac continued. 'In the book she's middle-aged and basically quite good-hearted although, in all honesty, I think she'd drive me right up the wall. She never stops talking and most of what she says is nonsense yet the characters in the book are all supposed to take pity on her. Her family were once well off but, at the time that the novel's set, they've become quite poor. Now, Miss Bates has a mother and she's a very interesting character. She's in quite a few scenes and is talked about a lot but I don't think she ever says a word.'

'Why is that?' Leigh asked.

'Well, Jane has it that she's deaf but I think that she just doesn't bother because she'd never get a word in edgewise anyway.'

'So, what has this Miss Bates and her mother got to do with the case?' Leigh asked with a puzzled expression.

'I'm hoping I'll find that out very soon,' Mac said mysteriously.

At the Police HQ they eventually found their way to the evidence store where Mac was handed a cardboard box. He was warned that nothing could be taken away but documentary evidence could be copied if required.

He sat down and opened the box. It consisted mostly of documents. One was a bank statement that showed that when she died Miss Hatch had a very healthy balance and, in that way at least, she was very far from being like Miss Bates. He looked at the statement carefully and the only outgoings he could see were quite mundane, energy, food, council tax and so on. There was one debit that interested him though. It appeared to be for an item of clothing from a Jane Austen gift shop, for the ill-fated ball he concluded.

There were only two further items that interested Mac and they were both near the bottom of the pile. The first was a photocopy of Philippa Hatch's will. It was dated just a few months before her death. She left everything to a mental health charity under the proviso that it was used to help to combat loneliness. The second was a copy of her birth certificate. Mac read this carefully.

Mac was beginning to think that his hunch might just be right.

'She was adopted,' he said. 'Mr. and Mrs. Hatch weren't her real parents and perhaps that explains why Mrs. Hatch didn't seem to be that close to her own daughter.'

'Who were her real parents then?' Leigh asked.

'There's only the mother's name on the certificate, Elizabeth Margaret Allenby, aged fourteen. I wonder if she was one of those poor girls who were more or less forced to give their babies up for adoption.'

'Poor Miss Allenby, poor Miss Hatch. Still I don't see how this gets us any further,' Leigh said.

'You don't?'

'Well, we've not come across anyone with those names yet. I mean, even if she married, she'd still have the same first name, now wouldn't she?'

'Not necessarily, people change their names all the time,' Mac said. 'Come on, let's get back to the station.'

Mac explained his theory to Andy and Toni and they all started work. Andy and Toni went to the Hertfordshire Registration Office and chased anything they could find in the records on Elizabeth Margaret Allenby. Meanwhile, Mac and Leigh started contacting all the local adoption agencies. They met up again three hours later.

'We've found Elizabeth Margaret Allenby, there's a marriage certificate...'

'I'll bet that she married someone called Corning,' Mac said.

Andy smiled.

'You're dead right there. She married John Corning in 1976 and they had a daughter, Jennifer Corning, two years later.'

'Did she change her first name then or something?' Leigh asked.

'Not really,' Mac replied. 'Peggy's short for Margaret but it's not a name you hear much these days. It's also not unknown for people to use their middle names if they don't like their first name that much. Do we have an address for the daughter?'

'Not yet,' Andy replied. 'There's no record of a Jennifer Corning living in the area so they're looking for a marriage certificate for her. We know that she's divorced so she still might be using her husband's name. What did you find out Mac?'

'We've found the adoption agency that Philippa Hatch used to trace her birth mother. They told us that through them she'd tried to contact her mother, twice as it turned out. Both times the reply was that her mother didn't want to be contacted. The second reply arrived on the morning of the ball.'

'So that's why she was so upset when Catherine kept going on about her mother,' Leigh interjected excitedly.

'She said in her suicide note that she'd been lonely for too long,' Mac said. 'She was obviously desperate and had placed all her hopes in getting a positive reply, so it wasn't Catherine but the fact that she thought her own mother didn't want to know her that killed her. Catherine just reminded her of the fact.'

'Tell me what you think happened,' Andy asked.

'Okay, Leigh you remember that Peggy's reason for joining the group was because her daughter was mad

165

on Austen and she wanted to know more about the novels?' Mac asked.

'Yes, that's what she was supposed to have said.'

'However, the daughter she was talking about wasn't Jennifer but Philippa. I'll bet that sometime after Philippa killed herself Peggy contacted the adoption agency herself and found out that her daughter had died. She must have felt tremendously guilty when she heard the news, perhaps she thought that joining the group and learning about Philippa's favourite author might be a way to get to know her dead daughter a little better. She was present when Anne described how Catherine had seemingly upset Philippa at the ball, upset her to such a degree that she killed herself shortly afterwards. Guilt can be a terrible thing and I think that it may have driven Peggy Corning to kill.'

'Yes, it all fits so far,' Andy said. 'There's still the thallium though?'

'That's something that my theory can't explain at the moment,' Mac said, 'but I'd bet that we'll find something when we have a look around where she lives. I've got the address that the adoption agency had on their records, we can try that.'

They were interrupted by a detective who gave Andy a sheet of paper. He showed the paper to Mac.

'That's the same address that I've got,' Mac said.

'Jennifer Corning is now called Jennifer Williams and...' he went to a large map pinned to a board, 'she lives here.'

Andy pointed at the map with his finger.

'Why that's right at the back of Amanda's house!' Mac exclaimed.

'I'll get a couple of uniforms and I'll meet you there in fifteen minutes,' Andy said as he disappeared down a corridor.

Mac and Leigh waited in the car a little down the road from Jennifer Williams' house. Mac gazed at the house but there was nothing different about it when compared to the rest of the Letchworth cottage-style homes that lined both sides of the road. It was just another two-storied building with a peaked roof, rendered and painted white. It was a bit larger than most but, otherwise, it was entirely unremarkable.

'So why exactly do you think she did it?' Leigh asked.

'Everyone has their breaking point and, as I said, guilt can be a terrible thing,' Mac replied. 'In those days I'll bet that she was made to feel guilty for having a child in the first place and then afterwards felt even more guilty for giving it up. She's carried that guilt around for over forty years now. Then, after refusing to meet her own daughter twice, she finally decides to contact her and she's told that her daughter's taken her own life. I think that might send anyone a little mad.'

'When you put it like that, I think I can see what you mean.'

Their conversation was terminated by the arrival of Andy and Toni in an unmarked car closely followed by a police car. Mac got out of the car as two uniformed officers made their way to the front door. He could hear the bell ringing inside but there was obviously no-one at home.

He turned and saw a woman in her late thirties coming towards the house. She had a house key ready in her hand and a look of fear on her face. The look of fear was intensified when Andy showed her his warrant card.

'Is it mum? Has something happened to mum?' she asked urgently.

'No, as far as we know your mother's alright,' Andy reassured her. 'I take it that you're Jennifer Williams, nee Corning?'

Fear was replaced by puzzlement.

'That's right. What do you want with me?'

'It's your mother we're looking for, routine enquiries that's all. Is she around?' Andy asked.

She opened the door.

'Come on, we may as well talk inside.'

She looked left and right to see if any of the neighbours were looking as she opened the door. They followed her into the living room.

'Mum won't be back from work for half an hour or so.'

'She's working?' Andy asked. 'Where?'

'At the Arts Café in town. She usually does three afternoons there a week. Can you tell me what this is all about?'

'I'm afraid not,' Andy replied. 'Is it okay if we have a look around?'

'I suppose so,' she replied with some hesitation.

Mac made straight for the back door. He unlocked it and went out into the garden. A few yards from the house there stood a brick outhouse. Some might have called it a shed but Mac thought it was a bit too substantial for that. The door was held shut by a rusty padlock.

'Look,' Mac said, pointing to the bottom of the door. It was open by at least an inch.

'More than enough for a squirrel to get through I'd have thought,' Andy said. 'Shall I ask for the keys or...'

He left the question hanging. Mac smiled and took out his lock picks. Although the lock looked rusty it opened easily enough. Mac knew why when he looked at the picks, they were smeared with oil.

'Someone's had this open recently,' Mac said.

Inside ranks of shelves ran around three sides of the outhouse, all were full of glass containers of different sizes and colours. Labels, somewhat faded now, gave the name of the substance and below that its chemical formula. Underneath the shelves and running the entire length of the wall opposite the door there was a wooden work bench that had three rows of fitted drawers

168

underneath. On the worktop he could see two Bunsen burners and several glass retorts and test tubes nestled in wooden racks. The surface was burned and scarred in places. All of the surfaces were dusty and strewn with cobwebs.

'Well, we were talking about chemical labs, it looks like we found one,' Andy said.

'It hasn't been used for some time though, has it?' Mac said. 'Except possibly for this.'

Mac pointed to a large container that was less than half full of a white powdery substance. The label said 'Thallium Sulphate TI2 SO4'. The lid had been cleaned of dust and it could be seen that the container had been moved from its original position.

'I'll bet that there'll be some good prints on that,' Mac said.

'And here look,' Andy said.

On one of the shelves the last of a row of red packets lay on its side. A red powder had spilled out, the packet having clearly been gnawed at by something.

'Your squirrel I'll bet,' Andy said. 'I'll get forensics in here as soon as possible. Let's go and see if Mrs. Corning's returned yet and see what she has to say.'

Mac pointed to other containers as they left.

'Strychnine, Arsenic, Atropine...there's enough poison to kill half of Letchworth. What in God's name was going on in here?'

Mrs. Corning still hadn't arrived and everyone was standing around awkwardly in the living room when Andy and Mac returned.

'What do you know about the outhouse?' Mac asked.

Jennifer Williams looked surprised.

'Dad's lab? Nothing really, Mum always kept it locked. No-one's been in there since he died as far as I know.'

'What did your dad do in there?' Mac asked.

She shrugged.

169

'I've no idea, he never talked about it and neither did mum. She'd only say that it was his little hobby. When he got ill, he spent even more time in there. Mum said it helped him to forget that he was dying.'

'What did he die from?'

'Luekaemia,' she replied. 'I was only eleven when he died. Unfortunately, they couldn't do much about it in those days.'

They all turned at the sound of a key in the front door lock.

A woman walked in and said, 'Hello Jenny, you'll never guess…'

She stood frozen for a few seconds at the sight of the police filling up her living room. Then her shoulders slumped and a half smile of resignation appeared on her face.

'You know,' she flatly stated.

'We do,' Andy replied. 'Mrs. Corning, we'd like you to accompany us to the station for questioning.'

'Of course. I suppose that it's just as well that I didn't take my coat off,' she said with a broad smile.

A murderess she might well be but Mac's first impressions of Peggy Corning were quite favourable. Her daughter looked from her mother to Andy and back again in sheer bewilderment.

'What does he know mum?' she asked. 'And why do you have to go to the police station? I was going to start cooking tea soon….'

'Don't worry about doing tea tonight, love,' Peggy Corning said as she turned to Andy. 'Can she come? She might as well hear it all at first hand.'

'If you like,' Andy replied.

He left one uniformed policeman guarding the front door and another outside the outhouse. The van containing the forensics team pulled up and Andy had a quick word with them.

Mother and daughter went to the station in Andy's car. In an interview room Andy and Mac sat opposite Peggy Corning and her daughter. Toni and Leigh watched the interview on CCTV. Peggy had refused to have a solicitor and seemed quite anxious to tell them her story.

'I knew that you'd find out and, if I'm honest, I'm quite relieved. It's been like waiting for the other shoe to drop. I'll say up front though that I'm glad that the bitch is dead and that she died in pain.'

'So, you admit to poisoning and killing Catherine Gascoigne?' Andy asked

Her daughter's brow furrowed in puzzlement.

'Who is Catherine Gascoigne, mum and why would you want to poison her? He's just joking, isn't he? Mum, please say that this is all some sort of joke.'

Peggy turned towards her daughter and gripped her hand tightly.

'It's no joke love but hush and listen and you'll hear the whole story.' She turned to Andy and said, 'Yes I poisoned her and I've no regrets about it either. Here's what happened…

I had Philippa when I was only fourteen. I didn't want her at the time, I'd been raped you see, raped repeatedly by my own father. I was bound to get pregnant sooner or later. So, they took her away and the good thing was that they took me away from my father too. I spent the next three years in a children's home and it was blissful compared to the life I'd been living.'

Mac glanced over at Jenny Williams. Her eyes were wide with surprise. This was obviously all news to her.

'So, I forgot all about Philippa, I made myself forget, until I had you love.'

She gently touched the side of her daughter's face.

'You were so beautiful, so innocent and then I thought about the baby I'd given up. She'd been innocent too, hadn't she? I mean it wasn't her fault she was born. So, as Jenny here grew up, I started thinking how old Philippa would be and I'd fantasise about what she'd look like and what she'd be doing. I prayed every day that they'd found her a good home and that she was happy. I eventually went to an adoption agency and talked to someone there. I thought about what they said to me and decided that I'd wait for her to contact me as they advised but she never did.'

Jenny tried to say something but her mother stopped her.

'Just let me say it all now love, no more secrets. I went to the agency again and that's when they told me that Philippa had died. They didn't say how though, I had to try and find that out for myself but I didn't even know where to start. I went to the library for some advice and I asked the librarian about how I could find out more about a death. She asked me for the details and, when I told her Philippa's name, I could see a look of surprise on her face.'

'I take it that this is Anne Holding that you're talking about?' Andy prompted.

'Yes, it was Anne. She was very kind to me that day. We went and had a coffee together. I didn't tell her that I was Philippa's mother though, I told her that I was a third cousin or something and I was doing some family research. She told me as gently as she could that Philippa had committed suicide but no-one seemed to know exactly why. She also told me of Philippa's love for Jane Austen and all about the Society. I didn't know anything about Jane at the time but I did love Pride and Prejudice when it was on the telly. I asked about the Society and if I could join but, from what Anne told me, they didn't sound like the type of people I'd get on with. Then she mentioned that she had her own little group and asked if I'd like to come and try it out.

So, I went and I thought they were all lovely and learning more about Jane's books made me feel a little

172

closer to Philippa. Then one evening, when the meeting was at Diane's, we'd all had a glass of wine too many and Anne told us about the last time she'd seen Philippa and how Catherine had bullied the poor girl into suicide. I'd finally found out what had caused my daughter to take her own life and, in that moment, I knew that I had to do something about it. It was the very least I owed her.

It was then that I remembered something that my husband had once said about thallium. He'd said that it was odourless and tasteless, the poisoner's poison he'd called it. I hadn't opened his shed since the day he'd died but I found the thallium easily enough. My husband had been very meticulous when it came to labelling his chemicals. The only problem was I wasn't sure of how much to use, so I just guessed. Catherine and some of her cronies used to visit the café I work in every week so I put some in her coffee, obviously not enough as she was still walking around the day afterwards. I tried again the next week, a little more this time, but it still didn't finish her off. I started watching her and when I saw that she regularly ran along the same route I came up with the idea of swapping her water bottle for one filled with a higher concentration of thallium but she still wouldn't die. Afterwards I could only think it was because she hadn't drunk it all.

Then, one day when Molly was telling us about how cruel Catherine had been to her, she let it slip about how easy it was to get into Catherine's house. She told us all about the key under the stone and her burglar alarm code being 4-3-2-1. So, I decided that this time I was going to make absolutely sure that she got the right dose. I watched her when she went out one morning and then located the key and got a copy made. Then a few nights later I went to her house.

I brought a hammer with me just in case she put up a fight but it was easy, so easy. She lay on the bed like a baby and was utterly defenceless as I poured the poison down her throat. I felt nothing, all I could see while I did it was my poor Philippa hanging by her neck. She was now finally getting some justice. I knew someone would find out eventually that it was me but I thought I should spend as much time with Jenny as I could in the meantime. So, there you have it.'

She smiled brightly at the two men opposite her.

'If you felt so protective about your daughter why did you refuse to meet with her not once but twice?' Andy asked.

She looked mystified.

'No dear, Philippa never contacted me, not once, never mind twice. I'd been hoping for years that she would but then I thought perhaps she's happy with her life and she doesn't need me. I waited for her to contact me but she never did.'

'Yes, she did, twice. The adoption agency showed us the records,' Andy stated.

'No, they must be wrong dear, I'd never turn my back on my own daughter, never!' she said fiercely.

Andy continued, 'The morning of the ball Philippa received a letter from the adoption agency where you stated for the second time that you didn't want any contact with her. Catherine Gascoigne at the ball talked to her as a character from the novel, a character that had a mother she was very close to. Catherine didn't bully her, at least not intentionally. She had Asperger's and probably couldn't see that your daughter was getting upset. She'd unintentionally rubbed salt into an open wound but we think it was the letter that made your daughter kill herself.'

Peggy looked absolutely mystified. Mac had been watching Jennifer closely during this exchange and thought he now had the answer.

'Perhaps someone answered for you. Tell me who deals with all the post in your house?' he asked.

'Why Jenny does, don't you dear? She's a secretary you know so...'

Peggy stopped in mid-sentence and looked at her daughter with something near horror.

'You didn't love, please Jenny say you didn't.'

All the colour drained from her daughter's face as she said, 'I was so sure that it was a mistake. I didn't want to upset you with it so I just replied and said that they'd got the wrong person. You always said that there were never had any secrets between us, you always said that, didn't you mum? It was always it was just you and me against the world, that's what you used to say. No secrets except for the fact that I had a sister of course. Oh God mum what have I done? I didn't mean...'

She burst into tears. Peggy hugged her daughter hard.

'It wasn't you love, not you, it was all my fault. I should have told you but I just couldn't. Shame is such a terrible thing, isn't it? As an adult I used to look at young girls and say to myself that I'd just been a kid at the time too, so how could any of it be my fault? It didn't stop me feeling ashamed though, it's something that stains your very soul.'

Still holding her daughter, she turned her head towards Andy as what he'd said just seemed to sink in.

'You're telling me now that Catherine was blameless? May God forgive me, keeping my dirty little secret to myself has killed two innocent people.'

Her face crumpled and tears raced down her cheeks too. The two women hugged each other and Mac felt an intense sorrow knowing that they'd soon be parted and probably for life.

Andy then formally charged Peggy Corning and left Toni to take her statement.

In the corridor he turned and shook Mac's hand.

'Another result but I have to admit that I don't take the least bit of pleasure from it.'

175

'Yes, I know justice must be done but who's to really blame here?' Mac said. 'If I thought that someone was responsible for killing my daughter then I honestly don't know what I'd do, then to find out that it was keeping her secret that had really caused it all.'

'Anyway, who'd have thought that finding a dead squirrel would lead to all this?' Andy said.

'Life can be so bloody strange at times,' Mac conceded.

Andy looked at his watch, it had just gone four-thirty.

'After all that I really need a drink. Is it too early for a pint?'

'It's never too early for a pint,' Mac stated with utter certainty.

'I'm in,' Leigh said.

One of the detectives called Andy over and spoke to him.

'Sorry Mac, is it okay if I join you in an hour or so?' Andy asked. 'Toni should be free by then too.'

As he and Leigh walked the short distance to the Magnets Mac couldn't help wondering how Philippa Hatch might have turned out if she'd have been born to different parents. Life can be such a lottery and unfortunately some people are given a losing ticket the second they're born.

He suddenly thought of Tim who he'd been neglecting recently. He rang and Tim said he'd meet them in half an hour. He had a bit of French polishing to finish off.

He looked at Leigh as she returned with the drinks. He thought now might be a good time to find a few things out.

'Do you mind if I ask you a couple of questions?'

She thought about it for a moment.

'No. I don't suppose so,' she said uncertainly.

'What's your real first name?'

'What!' she exclaimed with a surprised smile.

'I suspected when you first introduced yourself that Leigh wasn't your real name. I figured that you might be one of those people who've been called something embarrassing by their parents. Am I right?'

'And there was me on my first day thinking that I'd been landed with a right old duffer. You're right, Leigh isn't the name on my birth certificate.'

Mac gave her a big smile.

'Come on then, what is it?'

She looked up to the ceiling and then heaved a huge sigh.

'My bloody mother! Oh, I really love her and all that but I don't think I ever really forgave her for calling me... Kylie.'

Mac couldn't help laughing.

'Kylie? Really? That name definitely doesn't suit you.'

'That's what I thought too. She was a big fan of Kylie Minogue, still is, and she still calls me Kylie now even though I've had my name changed by deed poll. I've got my big brother to thank for the name I use now. He knew I hated Kylie so he cut it down and started calling me Lee instead and I thank him every day for it. When I changed my name, I changed the spelling to Leigh, it looked a little more feminine I suppose. I'd be really grateful if you kept this to yourself though.'

'Don't worry your secret's safe with me,' Mac said.

'You said you had two questions?' Leigh prompted him.

Mac's face showed that this question was a bit more serious.

'Yes. Tell me, just how bad was it at your last station?'

She gave him a startled look but said nothing.

Mac went on.

'I'd assumed that Monday had been your first day as a detective and I thought that was why you were being so skittish. However, you knew far more about the job than a new starter would know and that, plus Andy letting you out by yourself, gave me the idea that you'd been a detective somewhere else before coming here. You were being very defensive about everything so I also figured that it couldn't have been an altogether positive experience.'

She gave him a sad look.

'You can say that again. I worked on the beat in East London and, once I made detective, I worked out of the same station. I was the only woman and the rest of the team were mostly middle-aged men. The DI was a bastard, one of those men who like women but only if they're naked and in a magazine. He was always making little comments, comments that could be taken two ways if you know what I mean. Of course, the rest of the team followed his lead and would laugh their stupid heads off. The worst of it was that by the end they'd almost convinced me that it was my fault, that I was being too thin-skinned. They'd brag about the women they'd shagged and then, when I made it clear that I'd sooner be nailed to a tree than go to bed with any of them, they spread it around that I was a lesbian. I'm not though.'

'It shouldn't matter a damn if you were,' Mac said with feeling. 'I'm sorry for you but unfortunately I've come across too many coppers like that myself. They confuse being macho with being a good copper. I was lucky, when I took the murder team over my boss had already weeded out that type long before.'

'Anyway, I came here expecting more of the same I suppose but it's not the same is it?' she said.

'I'd hope not. Andy's a good copper and his heart's definitely in the right place.'

'If I'm honest I also thought that I was going to be the only woman on the team again,' she said. 'Then I met Toni. When I first heard her name, I just assumed that she'd be a man. We've had some good chats. She's very nice.'

'So, what do you think of it now?' Mac asked.

'I'm beginning to think that I made the right decision in coming here,' Leigh said with a smile.

'I think you probably did as well. I had to move too you know. I was a copper in Central Birmingham before I joined the Met. There's something about not being from the place that you're policing, I think you can be a bit more objective and see things that the locals hardly notice.'

'So why did you make the move?' she asked.

Mac spotted Tim striding up the hill and smiled.

'Stick around. It's a really good story and one day I'll tell you all about it.'

Yet another poisoning

This one was very special. He'd seen his next project on the television smirking and laughing. None of his victims were laughing though.

Another financial scam but this time ordinary people had been affected. Houses had burnt down, homes had been robbed, husbands and wives had died and, after years paying their premiums, people were now told that they weren't covered. This had just happened to a neighbour of his, a good friend. This was a scam too far in his opinion. It was giving the insurance business a bad name.

He decided that Mr. T was far too good for this one. Something a little stronger was required.

He knew his days were numbered so he'd had to prioritise his operations a little. However, there was no doubt in his mind who was number one on his list. He'd watched his victim carefully. He was a whisky drinker, which was good, and another good thing he'd noticed was that, when the division bell rang, he'd knock back whatever he had left in his glass before marching off to vote.

He knew he'd just have to bide his time and wait. He'd bought a large Macallen whisky and had added the secret ingredient. It would make it taste bitter so he didn't want his victim to just sip it. He waited until finally the bell rang and then he quickly switched glasses. He'd been careful to hold the glass using a paper napkin so he wouldn't leave any prints. The man didn't even look, he just grabbed the glass, knocked it back and made towards the door.

He waited a few moments before quietly making his way out of the building. The special ingredient would only take fifteen minutes or so to start working and he knew with some certainty that his victim wouldn't even make it to the hospital. He just wished that he'd been there to witness it though, the vomiting, the convulsions and the body spasms. It would not be an easy death. He had robbed vulnerable people and then smirked about it.

He deserved no better.

Chapter Eighteen

Four days later

Mac was once again sitting in his office and waiting for something to happen. His pulse quickened when he heard a heavy tread in the hallway and Andy Reid opened the door. It had been four days since Peggy Corning's confession.

'How are you keeping Mac?' Andy asked.

'I'm fine apart from being bored stiff. When I heard your footsteps, I said a little prayer that this is going to be a bit more than just a social visit.'

Andy smiled.

'I was hoping you'd say something like that. Have a look at this,' he said as he passed him a small black notebook. It looked quite old and battered.

'What is it?' he asked as he riffled through the pages.

Each page was written on, a clear hand using a fountain pen with blue ink. The ink had somewhat faded now.

'Forensics found it in one of the drawers in John Corning's lab. We've all had a quick look but none of us can make head or tail of it. However, for some reason I think it could be important. Also, you weren't too far wrong when you said there were enough chemicals in that shed to poison half of Letchworth. Forensics said that they've never had to remove such a large quantity of highly toxic material from a residential property before. Apparently, this John Corning really knew what he was doing from what they've told me. But why was he doing it? Even when he was dying, he kept on working in his lab. It's got me really intrigued. Unfortunately, this isn't a case as such so I can't put any police resource into it.'

'What's John Corning's background?' Mac asked.

'He did a degree in Chemistry with Maths and got a first but apparently the maths won and he ended up working as an actuary for an insurance company.'

'So, he was a trained chemist. I suppose he used the lab to keep his hand in but I agree there might be something else going on. I'll have a look. Did you ask Peggy Corning what her husband used to get up to in the shed?'

'Yes, I asked her but she said absolutely nothing,' Andy replied. 'She'd talk about anything else but, in all the interviews, the only thing she said about her husband was that he was a good man. That was it.'

'It looks like it's up to me then,' Mac said with a grin.

After Andy had gone, he looked carefully at each page. While some of the early ones had what looked like chemical notations and random notes, it was the later entries that looked more interesting. They all had the same structure. That structure consisted of something that almost looked like letters and numbers but they made no immediate sense to Mac. If it was a true code then he was sunk, he was no expert in codes. However, if its function was that of a record or memory aid then it might be some sort of shorthand.

He'd actually kept a little notebook like this himself before the age of computers and found that, to save time, he invented his own shorthand. He hoped that this was going to be something along those lines. He decided to start on the first page and concentrate on that. It almost looked like it was in a foreign language at first and it being handwritten didn't help. However, he eventually realised from the justification that he might be looking at mirror writing. He'd seen it once in a case some fifteen years before.

He locked up the office and went home. He got his laptop fired up and placed his shaving mirror on the table. While he was looking at the page from the notebook in the mirror, he entered what he saw on to the computer –

ARW cm
Ickst sc w t 6-8
L – Sol n19 L
W-bk bwy mf 9-5
b/o sw cc mgts f 8-10 p gl / or tr s 12-1 h gl
jd 17/7 TI2 SO4
aobtd

At least now it looked a little more familiar. He decided to try and decipher the bits he could. Looking at 'Ickst' he wondered if this could be 'Ickleford Street'. This was the street that Mac went down to get to the town centre in Letchworth. He made a note. Except for the formula for Thallium Sulphate the rest made no immediate sense. The numerals '6-8' and '9-5' suggested times but there was also a 17/7 – a date perhaps?

It was the final sequence of letters that bugged Mac as he was sure that he'd seen it before. He Googled the term and soon had his answer 'another one bites the dust'. He wondered if the late Mr. Corning had been a Queen fan. Whatever he was Mac was beginning to get a bad feeling about the notebook. 'ARW' made Mac think that this must relate to a person as they were capitalised. He wondered if someone with the initials ARW might have been poisoned on the 17th July. If this was the case then it had to be 1989 or before as John Corning had died in December 1989.

Mac did some digging on the internet and found that archived copies of one the local papers were kept at a library in Baldock. He decided to start there. He rang the library and they said that the information was held on microfilm but, if he wanted to give them half an hour, then they'd set it up for him. At the library a helpful young lady showed to him to an oversized, clunky looking machine with a large screen.

'It's getting on a bit now, all optics rather than digital but it's the only way we can view microfilm at the moment,' she explained.

She showed him how to move the film backwards and forwards and how to zoom in and out before she left him to it.

The roll of microfilm covered the Letchworth and Baldock Citizen newspaper for the years 1980-1991. He eventually found the edition covering the 17th July 1989 and read the death notices carefully. Nothing. He read the edition for the week afterwards. There was no-one with the initials ARW or even AW.

He rolled back to the previous year and tried again. Again, there was nothing for the 17th July edition or the weeks afterwards. He was beginning to wonder if he was on the right track. Then he looked at the 1987 editions and had no more luck. However, in the edition for the twenty third of July 1986, his eyes were immediately drawn to –

'Letchworth on July 19th 1986 after a short illness Arthur Reginald Wordsworth of Sollershott North. Dearly beloved husband of Helen. The funeral will be held at St. Thomas Church at 11 am on 25th July followed by interment at Wilbury Hills Cemetery. No flowers please.'

Mac looked at his laptop. The notice explained another part of the puzzle. 'L – Sol n19 L', it probably meant 'Lived – 19 Sollershott North, Letchworth.'

It was a long shot but he decided to Google the name and was surprised when he got several recent results. Wordsworth's name had cropped up as part of a police investigation into historic child abuse allegations in Hertfordshire called Operation Alder. On the surface he seemed to be a respectable man, manager of a local bank and a scout leader but in private he was part of a predatory paedophile ring that also included other 'respectable' men including a couple of police officers. One of these was still alive and was currently facing prosecution.

Mac looked at his notes. He worked in a bank and that might explain the next line 'W-bk bwy mf 9-5' which might mean 'Worked – Bank, Broadway, Monday – Friday 9-5'. The note seemed to be a précis of a person's life, where he lived and where he worked. Mac needed to know more.

He now had an idea of what 'Ickst sc w t 6-8' meant, 'Ickleford Street Scouts Wednesday and Thursday 6-8' and the 'cm' next to the initials could be 'child molester'. It also occurred to Mac what 'jd 17/7' might mean 'job done 17/7'.

This just left the line 'b/o sw cc mgts f 8-10 p gl / or tr s 12-1 h gl' to explain. He now knew that 'f 8-10' and 's 12-1' probably referred to days and times but he'd need to give the rest some thought.

He picked another page at random. Using the shaving mirror again he got this –

MV wb
L – Sum r 94 L
W- m gar, wks r m-sat 8-5
b/o b newc br way home
jd 19/11 TI2 SO4
aobtd

Mac knew from this that someone with the initials MV lived at 94 Summer Road, Letchworth. They worked in Works Road Monday to Saturday eight until five and, as this was mostly an industrial area, Mac guessed that 'gar' probably meant 'garage'. They were killed on 19th November again using thallium.

The fourth line interested Mac most as it gave him a really good clue as to its meaning. 'Newc br' could only mean Newcastle Brown and the 'b' must then mean 'bottle' which was the only way it was sold anyway. 'Way home' did this mean on the way to the victim's or John Corning's home? Mac couldn't be sure. What he was fairly sure of now was what b/o meant – 'best opportunity'.

He looked again at the same line in the first note. He now understood that this line related to the modus operandi for the killings. It still took him a fair amount of thinking to arrive at a reasonable guess - 'b/o sw cc mgts f 8-10 p gl / or tr s 12-1 h gl' might mean 'Best opportunity swap coca-cola Magnets Fridays 8-10 pint glass / Orange Tree Sundays 12-1 half glass.'

The poisoner was noting where and when the victim drank and also what they drank, presumably so that he could buy exactly the same. It was simple, just add the thallium and then swap glasses.

He decided to take a punt and go to 94 Summer Road. A woman in her sixties answered the door.

'Yes dear?' she asked.

He introduced himself.

'I'm helping the police out with an enquiry. How long have you been living here?'

The woman thought for a moment.

'A long time dear, it must be well over thirty years now.'

Mac felt like he'd just put his week's wages on an outsider and it had come in first.

'Can I ask you what your name is?'

'Maureen Caulderwell, dear,' she replied. 'Won't you come in?'

She showed him into a comfortable, warm living room.

'Cup of tea, dear?' she asked.

Mac found he was thirsty.

'Yes, please.'

While she was making the tea, he ran his eyes along a mass of framed photos that covered the top of a large sideboard. Most of them were of her with two boys. From the earlier pictures it was clear that one was about six or seven years older than the other although as they got older this disparity wasn't so obvious. A few were of Maureen and a man of about the same age. His eyes lit up when he saw one of Maureen with two women, one of which was definitely a young Peggy Corning.

'Looking at my photos, dear. I find them a real comfort, they remind me of all the good times,' she said cheerily.

'Do you know anyone with the initials MV who might have lived here in the eighties?' Mac asked.

The smile abruptly left her face.

'Yes, that would be my first husband, Mike Vaughan.'

'What happened to him?' Mac asked.

'Oh, he died dear and it couldn't have happened to a nicer person.'

'What do you mean?' Mac asked.

'I was an idiot when I was young,' she said. 'Mike was good looking, a bit of a bad lad too but I didn't realise then just how much badness he really had in him. He was drunk all the time towards the end. He was working and I was too but every penny we earned got spent on drink.'

A little look of shame crossed her face.

'He used to knock me around sometimes too, quite a lot towards the end but it was when he started on Eddie, our son, that I started dreaming about killing him. Eddie was only five at the time. Anyway, luckily I didn't need to bother as he died soon afterwards.'

'What did he die of?' Mac asked.

'The doctor thought it was probably the drink although he said that he couldn't be absolutely sure.'

'Was his favourite drink Newcastle Brown Ale by any chance?' Mac asked.

'I don't know how you could possibly know that but yes,' she said with some surprise. 'The first thing I used to have to do every morning was throw out his empties. I still hate seeing a bottle of the stuff nowadays, it brings it all back.'

'How did you know Peggy Corning?' Mac asked. 'I saw her in one of your photos.'

'I thought this might have something to do with Peggy, I heard all about the poisoning on the news. Tragic, dear. Anyway, I'll never say a bad word about Peggy, she really helped me just before Mike died. She was the only one I could talk to about it at the time.'

Mac would bet that Peggy might have also mentioned it to her husband.

'I saw a man in some of the photos...' Mac said.

'Yes, that's my husband Derek. You know I thought that all men must be like Mike, my dad certainly was, but Derek was different. He's always treated me like a queen he has. He took Eddie on as his own child and then we had another son Tom. They've been really good sons to us. They've both gone to university and got good jobs and they've got families of their own now.'

'It seems as if things have turned out really well for you,' Mac said.

'Yes, they did,' she replied with a smile. 'I know I shouldn't but I say a little prayer of thanks every day that God saw fit to take Mike when he did.'

However, Mac knew that it wasn't God but John Corning who had done the taking. He thanked her and said goodbye.

Sitting in the car he took the notebook out and leafed through it. He was especially interested in the line that contained the address. 'L' he knew meant Letchworth, there were a couple of 'St' entries, probably Stevenage, four or five 'H' entries, presumably Hitchin, and the majority of the rest were 'Ln' which Mac took as being London. One entry towards the end made him catch his breath. He drove home and got straight on his laptop.

He carefully noted down the entry using the shaving mirror –

L St W MP sw

L – Hpdn mnr hse

W –HoP

b/o str b smw macallan

jd 02/10 C21H22N2O2

aobtd

Whether it was because he'd now got a feeling for the way John Corning noted things down or because there were a couple of giveaways, 'MP' next to the initials and the full spelling of 'macallen', Mac wasn't sure.

He put 'Lawrence St. Winterley' in the search bar and then selected the Wikipedia entry. Mac remembered the case as it had caused quite a stir at the time. A sitting MP for one of the Hertfordshire constituencies had been suspected of being behind a countrywide insurance scam. However, evidence supporting this claim mysteriously disappeared from police custody and there was a big stink when it was discovered that St. Winterley had recently proposed the Chief Constable of the very same police force to be a member of a very exclusive gentleman's club. The papers started calling him the 'Teflon Toff' as nothing from his numerous and increasingly risky financial escapades ever seemed to stick. The insurance scam had been a bad one though, not just hitting wealthy investors who could afford to lose money, but many ordinary people who found they had no cover at all when a husband died or a house burnt down.

St. Winterley had been found collapsed in a side corridor at the House of Commons in London on the 3rd October 1989 and he died shortly before reaching hospital. The cause of death was established as strychnine poisoning. Mac guessed that it had been administered in a drink, Macallen whisky, in the Strangers Bar.

He wondered why John Corning had used strychnine and looked it up. Once taken the poison had no antidote and the victim only died after undergoing terrible muscle spasms and convulsions. He guessed that John Corning hadn't just wanted St. Winterley to die but to die in great pain too.

Mac had met many wrongdoers in his time, a few who he might even describe as being truly evil, but he'd always been happy to leave the judging and sentencing to others. John Corning had appointed himself as judge, jury and executioner and Mac felt there was something every bit as evil about that as anything his victims might have done.

He arranged to meet Andy at the station an hour or so before he was due to meet with Tim. His team, Aston Villa, had just got knocked out of the cup in the fifth round by a club some three divisions below them and a full inquest had to be held.

He gratefully passed the notebook back to Andy.

'So, did you find anything?' Andy asked.

'Too much,' Mac replied.

He picked out the page for Arthur Reginald Wordsworth and took him through the notes.

'You're joking! So, each one of these pages relates to a murder? How many are there?' Andy asked.

'I counted forty nine in all but I think that there were only forty eight murders as there's no 'job done' or 'another one bites the dust' on the last one. My bet is that he died before he could carry that one out.'

'Bloody hell, I still can't believe it,' Andy said. 'I'm holding a notebook belonging to Hertfordshire's biggest serial killer.'

'You'll never be able to prove it though, unless you can get Peggy Corning to testify, which I doubt in the extreme. John Corning was very clever and, after all this time, there's unlikely to be any evidence other than what's contained in this notebook.'

'Do you think that Peggy Corning knew about this?' Andy asked, his finger tapping the notebook.

'I'd guess that she didn't know everything that her husband was up to, probably because she didn't want to know. However, I think that she knew enough. One of the entries in the notebook relates to the husband of one of her friends. He was a drunk and a wife beater and, from what his ex-wife told me, it was a blessing to her when he died. I'd bet that Peggy Corning, at the very least, gave her husband a big hint that here was someone who didn't deserve to live.'

'Do you think it was being diagnosed with leukaemia that made him do it?' Andy asked.

Mac shook his head.

'He'd already committed eighteen murders by that time but it certainly accelerated his efforts, thirty murders in just over six months.'

He passed the notebook back to Andy.

'Thanks Mac,' Andy said. 'I know we probably can't do anything about it after all these years but somehow it's still good to know the truth.'

Andy stood up and shook hands with Mac.

'Do you mind if I call around if I need you or maybe just for a chat?'

'Please do, especially if you've got a case that you need some help with.'

As he walked towards the Magnets Mac thought about John Corning's little black book. He decided that life wasn't just weird but was often weirder than you could ever know.

'What a load of wasters!' Tim exclaimed with feeling as Mac arrived at table thirteen. 'I can't believe it. I really thought this year might be different. Oh well, there's just the league now but as we're fifth from bottom there's not much bloody hope there either. Anyway, I'll get them in.'

They spent the evening tearing their favourite football team apart and putting it back together again. It was definitely a more enjoyable experience than watching them play. While they were doing this, he looked over at Tim and thanked God that he was his friend.

In his research he'd come across one of Jane's quotes that had stuck in his head.

'*My idea of good company is the company of clever, well-informed people who have a great deal of conversation; that is what I call good company.*'

Mac looked over at his good friend. He couldn't have put it better himself.

Three months later -

'This is BBC Three Counties Radio with the news at five o'clock. The top story is that the four-week trial of local resident George Parker has ended. Mr. Parker, who is from Letchworth, has been found guilty of bribing foreign government officials and in aiding and abetting terrorists. Mr. Justice Haining said the charges were serious in the extreme and that the defendant knowingly funded terrorist organisations in order to gain contracts for his company. He warned Mr. Parker that he was facing a lengthy custodial sentence. Sentencing will take place next week.

On a somewhat lighter note we can report that a local woman who recently died has left just over six and a half million pounds to a local group of Jane Austen fans. The Letchworth Society of Janeites were bequeathed the money by Mrs. Catherine Gascoigne in order to provide a permanent base for students and others researching nineteenth century literature and also to hold a bi-annual international conference.

Mrs. Anne Holding, the chair of the Society, said that Mrs. Gascoigne's incredibly generous gift would be put to good use and that it would put Letchworth on the world map with regard to the study of authors such as Jane Austen, the Brontes and Elizabeth Gaskell. She announced that the conference centre, which is due to open in three years, would be named after Mrs. Gascoigne who has also bequeathed a further six million pounds to be split between a local autism charity and cancer research.

And now some news just in. It's been announced that a celebrity wedding took place this morning in the village of Willian near Letchworth. Billionaire financier Alix Stefanovic has re-married his ex-wife Diane. The couple famously split up in a very public and very acrimonious divorce that ended with Diane Stefanovic being awarded one of the biggest settlements ever by an American court. It's being reported that a wedding reception is being held at a secret location somewhere in Hertfordshire.

In other news a Stevenage man and his dog were found drunk in a...'

THE END

I hope you enjoyed this story. If you have then please leave a review and let me know what you think.

Also available in the Mac Maguire series

The Body in the Boot

The Weeping Women

The Blackness

23 Cold Cases

Two Dogs

The Match of the Day Murders

The Chancer

The Tiger's Back

The Eight Bench Walk

You can learn more about me and my books by visiting my author website -
https://patrickcwalshauthor.wordpress.com

Made in the USA
Columbia, SC
22 February 2025